MAUI ROSE

MAUI ROSE

•

ANNETTE MAHON

AVALON BOOKS

THOMAS BOUREGY AND COMPANY, INC.
401 LAFAYETTE STREET
NEW YORK, NEW YORK 10003

PRINTED IN THE UNITED STATES OF AMERICA
ON ACID-FREE PAPER
BY HADDON CRAFTSMEN, SCRANTON, PENNSYLVANIA

For George, my very own hero, for his faithful support.
And for Margo, Lindsey, and Cari Anne, for their unwavering enthusiasm.

Chapter One

The Kahului airport bustled with activity, the air heavy with afternoon warmth, tropical humidity, and the noisy exuberance of excited travelers. Amid the cheerful scramble, Dr. Lani Kalima searched frantically for a white-haired man. She was late—terribly late—meeting his plane. Could he have already picked up his luggage and left on his own? The warm, humid air, perfumed by the tropical blossoms of dozens of leis worn by arriving passengers, was beginning to make her head ache.

Finally, up ahead of her, she spotted a full head of white hair. As that gentleman turned and saw her, a wide smile made his dark eyes twinkle. Lani smiled in return, the sight of her associate banishing the incipient headache. She could tell just by looking at him that he'd enjoyed the week spent with his daughter and grandchildren. He looked rested and relaxed for the first time in months.

"Uncle Charles!" Lani placed the plumeria lei she held around his neck, depositing a kiss on his smooth cheek. His smile of pleasure at her simple gift made her glad she'd taken the time to make the lei, even though she'd had to get up an hour early to collect the flowers and skipped her lunch to string them.

The noise of the huge luggage carousel starting up distracted her just as she started to ask about his trip. Instead, Lani squeezed his arm. "You wait here, Uncle Charles. I'll get your bag."

Even before she finished speaking, Lani moved forward and wedged herself into a narrow space alongside the moving carousel. Just in time. Coming around the corner from the right was the dark gray, hard-sided suitcase that belonged to Uncle Charles.

Then everything seemed to happen at once. She caught a glimpse of another arm reaching for the same bag . . . and felt a sharp impact on her right shoulder. Already off-balance from reaching over the raised side of the carousel, Lani was thrown forward. She was falling—facefirst—toward the moving plates of the luggage carousel!

Just in time, a pair of large hands grasped her waist. The steady hands easily held her, preventing a catastrophic fall, then steadied her while she caught her balance. But not before the large shoulder bag she carried flew off her shoulder, hit the terminal floor with a crash, and tumbled its innumerable contents in all directions.

"Ohhh!" Lani was so surprised, she stood stock-still for a full five seconds before she had the presence of mind to turn to the cause of the accident. "Look what you've done!" she snapped at him in a frustrated voice as she dropped down, frantically reaching for items before they were stepped on or stolen.

She looked back up at him as she snatched up her wallet and keys, but he was just a looming shadow with a bright nimbus of outside light behind him. A very large shadow. Her eyes moved rapidly across the wide expanse of his body, watching him lean forward to remove the dark suitcase that had made its way around to them again. "And that's my suitcase you're holding."

Still grabbing at loose bits, thankfully accepting pens and lipstick and tissue packets from the strangers around her, Lani missed the speculative look he cast over her—from the top of her dark hair, down to her tiny feet in their practical white pumps.

"Actually, that's *my* suitcase." Lani heard Uncle Charles's voice coming from just above her. "Lani was just retrieving it for me."

"Oh, but it's mine."

A new voice, female, had entered the fray. Her things—all of them, she sincerely hoped—finally thrown back into her capacious bag, Lani thanked all her impromptu helpers and stood.

The new voice evidently belonged to a plump woman in her fifties standing beside the unmannerly giant who'd toppled Lani in the first place. The top of her head, with its reddish brown curls, was at least an inch short of the large man's shoulders.

"Oh, hello again." The woman's pale cheeks flushed a rosy pink as she caught sight of Charles. Then she stepped forward, her hand extended toward Lani in greeting, her brow furrowed in concern. "You must be Lani. I'm afraid it's all my fault. Derek was just getting my bag. I'm Barbara Wolfe, and I'm so sorry," she added.

Lani shook her hand automatically.

"The big oaf is my son, Derek," Barbara continued. "Apologize to the nice lady, Derek."

Lani hid a smile at the offhand way the older woman treated the large man beside her. He probably felt about two feet tall and all of six years old.

Now that she could actually see him, Lani realized Derek was extremely good-looking, and probably well into his thirties. It must be very embarrassing for him to be treated that way, yet he wasn't visibly affected by his mother's words.

And he *was* good-looking. In fact, he was just about the best-looking man she'd ever seen. His eyes were a smoky shade somewhere between blue and gray, his nose classic, though a bump along the length of it spoiled its perfection and probably indicated that it had been broken at some point in his life. His lips had the chiseled look of a Greek statue. And his body! He had the build of a highly trained athlete. Tall—at least an inch or two over six feet—broad in the chest and shoulders, he must easily weigh two hundred pounds, and every bit of it muscle.

The blood drained from her face. Derek Wolfe. Surely it wasn't *the* Derek Wolfe!

The area around them grew quiet as the other passengers retrieved their luggage and moved away. Unnoticed, a lone suitcase, dark gray and strikingly similar to the one now standing between Lani and Derek, continued to travel around and around on the carousel.

Derek looked down at the young woman standing before him. She wasn't his type. He'd always gone for tall, leggy blonds. Lani, although attractive, was tiny, with long, wavy black hair that she'd pulled away from her oval face with a large clip. Hers was a pretty face, with features as delicate as any porcelain doll's. She had large cat's eyes, so dark he couldn't distinguish the iris from the pupil, and the longest natural eyelashes he'd ever seen. And he'd swear they were natural, as she didn't appear to be wearing any makeup at all. But even without it, her skin was a warm golden brown with a natural, healthy glow, and her lips were a burnished cherry. With her petite build, she seemed delicate and fragile, yet he sensed there was a hidden strength in that lean, well-proportioned body.

He felt lucky to have caught her before she was injured in that fall. His darn unreliable knees! He could have been the cause of a serious injury, and all because he was too proud to let his mother retrieve her own suitcase. His body was no longer the perfect specimen he had taken for granted over the years—and his reluctance to admit it could have caused serious injury to this lovely young woman.

Derek and Lani studied each other in the glassy light of the airport terminal and sensed a current in the air that both wanted to disregard. If the air weren't so heavy with moisture, he'd swear it was static electricity. But under the circumstances, that wasn't a possibility.

Derek pulled his gaze from the face before him, looking for something to take his mind away from such fanciful thoughts. Having his mother back must already be making him crazy. Otherwise why would he be staring at a cute little stranger, thinking lyrical thoughts—burnished cherry indeed!

Barbara broke the mood when she began speaking again. ''Charlie and I were sitting together on the plane. How funny that our luggage should be the same.''

Derek mumbled something incoherent and turned to check the carousel again. Another dark gray suitcase was just rounding the corner toward them.

Meanwhile Lani stared at Barbara and Charles, surprise robbing her of speech. The idea that anyone would call old-fashioned, old-worldly Doctor Charles Wong ''Charlie''— and that he would appear to enjoy it! Well, it was almost too much to contemplate!

Lani remained silent while Derek busied himself matching the luggage checks with their respective stubs. Barbara chatted with them, unaware of Lani's jumbled thoughts.

''We had such fun talking on the plane,'' Barbara told Lani. ''We shared pictures of our grandchildren too.'' She turned to Charles, putting her hand lightly on his arm. ''I hope we can get together soon and continue our acquaintance.''

Charles smiled at her, covering her hand with his own. ''I hope we can. You know, I'm slowly turning my practice over to Lani here, so I have more time off these days. Maybe we can have lunch one day soon.''

Lani watched with interest. He really liked her! She smiled to see the two of them. It reminded her of her high school years; Charles and Barbara were like shy teenagers feeling each other out about a date.

Derek broke the mood for her when he stepped over with a suitcase. "This one is yours. Or rather, his." He nodded toward Charles. Then he looked back at her, running his hand through his hair before shoving both hands into his pants pockets. *Why, he's embarrassed,* Lani thought.

"I want to apologize about earlier. I didn't mean to knock you over that way." He looked down at the head that just barely cleared his shoulder, and decided he needn't mention his own physical limitations. "You're just so darn little, I didn't even see you."

Lani thought that if that was an apology, it left a bit lacking. Still, he'd tried. "That's okay. I know it was an accident." Then she drew herself up to her full five feet four inches. "And I'm not that little. I may not be tall, but I'm not short either."

Derek grinned at her, grateful to be off the hook for his thoughtless remark. "Let me guess. You're just right."

"Absolutely." Lani gave a wry smile. "Though you needn't make me sound like a bowl of porridge."

They were still laughing together when Barbara and Charles approached. "We're ready," Barbara announced. She held the tether of the second suitcase in her hand, though her son promptly took it from her. Lani noted the automatic gesture with approval. So maybe he wasn't the unmannerly oaf she'd first thought.

The four of them finally began to move off toward the parking lot. And just in time. Another wave of debarking passengers surged into the baggage claim area as they left.

Barbara and Charles said their good-byes with promises to meet again later in the week. Derek and Lani were careful not to say anything. Derek reminded himself that she wasn't his type. Lani kept asking herself, Derek Wolfe—is it *the* Derek Wolfe?

The lush green mountains of the Valley Isle flowed past on their right as Lani drove Charles toward home on the busy highway. To their left stretched the beautiful Maui shoreline, white sand beaches lapped by the clear blue sea. Fresh, sea-scented breezes blew in through the open windows as Lani concentrated on her driving. Uncle Charles, unusually talkative this afternoon, regaled her with stories about his grandchildren.

''That Amy is so smart. Only two, and you should hear her talk!''

As Charles paused, smiling in remembrance, Lani decided to forget subtlety and ask the question that had been niggling at her all the way from the airport.

''So you sat with Barbara Wolfe on the plane.''

Charles's smile grew even wider. ''Ah, yes. Such a nice woman. We talked the whole time.''

''Is her son the Derek Wolfe I've heard so much about?''

Charles looked over at her. Lani carefully kept her gaze on the road. ''Now, you aren't thinking about that incident at the luggage carousel, are you? That really was an accident, Lani. I saw it all from behind you two.''

''Oh, I know it was an accident, Uncle Charles. I just didn't place the name right away, and then I wondered if it really was him.''

''He was a big football star, if that's what

you mean.'' Charles grinned at her. ''He's a handsome guy, don't you think?''

In her peripheral vision, Lani caught sight of a surfer riding a small wave smoothly into shore. She'd like to pull over and park for an hour and do nothing but watch the waves break and the surfers try to ride them in. Just sit there and relax and not think about work, or finances, or anything.

But a young pediatrician trying to establish her practice couldn't afford that. Even if she had a wonderful honorary uncle like Charles Wong with an established practice to join.

Lani realized the silence had gone on for too long and hurriedly tried to remember what the question was. Derek was a handsome guy all right. For reasons she didn't want to look into, she just didn't want to admit it out loud. But she had to say something.

''He is a handsome man. But I've heard a lot of stories. . . .'' Her voice trailed off. She hated to admit having seen some of it in those supermarket tabloids.

''Oh, Barbara said you can only believe a tenth of the stories about him. She said she learned early not to believe anything at all until she'd talked to him.'' Charles shifted a little in the seat. "Must be hard having someone you love turn into a celebrity."

They were nearing their turnoff and Lani had to slow down. She used the small maneuver as an excuse to turn her full attention to the road, leaving that particular topic behind.

Charles picked up the conversational ball by remembering the cute way Amy pronounced "spaghetti." He continued to talk about her and her brother until they pulled into the driveway of the old house.

Chapter Two

It had been a hectic morning.

Having Uncle Charles back from the mainland last night after his first two-week vacation in years had demanded a celebratory dinner of sorts. So he and Lani lingered over their meal, talking until late about his trip and the joy he'd received from interacting with his grandchildren in their home environment.

Then she'd had to awaken early this morning; it was her day to drive out to the hospital in Wailuku to examine the newborns. It was always a joy to see the tiny new humans, to have a short visit with the happy mothers. But it did involve the long thirty-minute drive out to Wailuku—a whole hour lost on the road.

So she was already tired when she arrived at the office. Every baby and child in Lahaina seemed to have some type of respiratory infection—and was waiting in their office to see herself or one of her associates.

At ten past noon, with a sigh of relief, Lani closed the door on her last morning patient and headed to her office for a well-deserved lunch break. But it was not to be.

''Lani!''

Carolann, the receptionist, called for her before she'd taken two steps. Short, with dark brown skin, Carolann had an abundance of straight black hair that she wore in a long braid down her back. In her short flared skirt and a knit blouse, Carolann could easily pass for one of their older patients.

At the moment, she walked down the hall toward Lani with an apologetic expression.

''Someone's just come in with a little boy and his grandmother. The boy might have a broken ankle. But the grandmother's almost hysterical—upset that he got hurt while she was watching him. And the parents are scuba diving at Molokini.''

Lani sighed. Lunch had sounded good—actually, getting off her feet for an hour was what held the appeal. She could almost feel the soft leather of her comfortable chair, and the smooth wood of the small footstool where she placed her shoeless feet. . . .

But this was more important.

Rotating her shoulders to ease the weariness, Lani continued past her office door to the trauma room. It was one of the smaller examining rooms, fitted up for suturing and the making of casts; a large supply cupboard took up much of the room, making it smaller than the others.

Lani took the file from its holder on the door and glanced quickly over the information it contained. Then she entered the room.

The smile directed at the little boy on the examining table faltered as she glimpsed a large man taking up an inordinate amount of space in the small room. He was a tall, broad, extremely handsome man who proffered a wide grin when he saw her.

''Why, Dr. Kalima. It *is* you. Hello again.''

Derek Wolfe put his arm around the white-haired woman beside him and squeezed her shoulders. "I told you he'd be fine, Miriam. Dr. Kalima here is a great doctor. She'll take good care of Justin, won't you, Doctor?"

"Of course." Lani had to stifle an unruly chuckle. After all, what else could she possibly say to a loaded question like that?

Trying to ignore Derek Wolfe, an almost impossible task in the small room, Lani approached the young boy. The chart said he was five, but he was small for his age, with huge blue eyes that were currently water-logged. Fair wisps of baby-fine hair fluttered around his face whenever he moved his head.

Lani smiled at him, care and friendliness radiating from her. From his position beside Justin's grandmother, Derek could sense her sincerity and her desire to help the little boy. Justin seemed to feel it too. He quieted visibly at Lani's calmness, offering a wavery smile in return.

It was an experience watching her work.

From their brief meeting yesterday at the airport, Derek had known Lani was a beautiful woman. From his mother's long dissertation on their way home and throughout dinner, he'd learned something about her Uncle Charlie.

But apparently Charlie talked a lot about his wonderful niece who was taking over his practice so he could retire. According to his mother, who'd had it from Charlie, Lani was very smart, capable, and compassionate.

He'd told Justin she was a great doctor because Justin and his emotional grandmother had needed to hear it. But now, as he watched her deft examination of the child's leg and ankle, he knew he'd been correct. She did everything she needed to do to make a diagnosis, and she managed to keep the child chattering happily throughout. Even Miriam had settled down and finally stopped dabbing at her damp eyelids.

As she finished her examination, Lani looked over at the grandmother. She was an attractive woman now that she'd dried her tears and relaxed a little. Lani gave her an encouraging smile.

"He'll be fine. I don't think anything is broken. But we'll need an X ray of that ankle just to be sure. Carolann will call down to the Radiology Lab—it's two doors down."

Lani turned back to the little boy.

"We're going to take a picture of the bones in your foot, Justin. Okay?"

Justin nodded. "I know about X rays," he said.

Lani had to grin over at Derek. The little boy's voice said it all: they must think he was a dumb little baby not to know about X rays.

Lani took a sticker from a roll—it said "Great Patient" in neon bright colors—and stuck it onto the front of his T-shirt. "You've been a 'great patient,' Justin, just as this says." She smiled at him again before turning to Miriam. "Now, if you'll excuse me, I'll get Carolann to set up that appointment. She'll come and tell you when to go over."

With another smile she was gone. Derek looked after her, admiration evident upon his face.

Twenty minutes later, Derek found Lani in her office. Miriam and Justin were on their way to the radiologist's and he was free to go. But he found himself reluctant to leave without spending a little more time with Lani.

He put his head around the open door of her office. "Got a minute?"

Lani looked up, a half-smile on her face. Belatedly he noticed the phone receiver in her hand.

"Not really, but come on in anyway."

Derek came inside the small room and seated himself in one of the chairs across from her desk. "You were very good with Justin."

"Thank you. How did you happen to be with them? Is he a relative of yours?"

"Oh, no. I was just coming in to work when I saw Justin fall. He was skipping along beside his grandma and his foot just went out from under him." Though he wouldn't say as much to Lani, it was something Derek could definitely relate to. "He started screaming right away and Miriam was almost as bad." Derek shrugged. "I figured they needed one calm head among them. So I bundled them into the car and came here."

He saw her open her mouth, ready to ask a question.

"How did I know to come here?" he asked with a grin.

Lani laughed. "You not only know the answers but the questions. So by all means, go on." She pulled a small vinyl lunch bag from a desk drawer and reached inside. "If you don't mind, though, I do have to start my lunch. I have a lot of phone calls to return before we start seeing patients again at two o'clock.''

''Sure, go right ahead. I'd offer to take you out, but I know you don't have the time.'' He watched her open a plastic bag and remove a sandwich, wondering what she preferred. ''Good grief, is that a peanut butter sandwich?''

Lani stiffened at his incredulous tone. ''I like peanut butter.'' She took a small bite and chewed it quickly. ''And it's also economical and easy to prepare first thing in the morning.'' She took a sip from the can of guava juice she'd also taken from the bag. ''So . . . You were going to tell me how you knew about our office.''

Derek seemed properly chastised. ''Yes. Well . . .'' He ran his fingers through his honey-colored hair, throwing the thick mass into disarray. Lani had known someone in college with hair that wonderful shade of golden brown. He'd been very nice too, but not nearly as attractive.

Lani pulled her wandering thoughts back to the man before her as he began to speak again.

''Justin fell right near the restaurant. I know the people who work in the stores along there.

I asked Kanani, the woman who manages the gallery near where he fell. She came out to see what was going on when she heard all the noise. She told me about this place and gave me directions.''

Lani's brow furrowed at the name. She finished chewing the last of her sandwich and took a drink to wash it down. ''Kanani Shimazu?''

Derek smiled. ''Yeah. You know her?''

''She brings in her twins.''

Derek's eyebrows rose almost to his hairline. ''She has twins? Little Kanani?''

''She's not that little, and yes she has. They're three years old, a boy and a girl. You have a disconcerting way of calling people who are smaller than you little. Try to remember that you are taller than average.''

Derek squashed a tart reply, working to keep his expression bland. He *was* a big man, and he truly didn't mean to offend anyone. He'd have to watch his vocabulary.

Lani finished her juice and carefully placed the empty can on the corner of her desk. She saw Derek watching her and explained. ''We recycle the aluminum cans. I put it there to remind myself to take it out to the coffee room where the recycle bins are kept.''

Derek wasn't surprised to hear Lani's explanation. Although he barely knew her, she seemed like someone who would care about her environment and do something, however small, to help preserve it.

He fidgeted in the visitor's chair as she cleared away the remains of her simple lunch. He'd better talk fast. He sensed that she was getting ready to kick him out. Already she looked properly businesslike and serious.

''Lani,'' he began.

She turned her large, dark, sloe eyes on him and he found it necessary to clear his throat before continuing. She had the finest eyes he'd ever seen.

''I, ah, wanted to apologize for my behavior at the airport yesterday.''

Lani's face mirrored her surprise. ''You don't have to apologize. I know it was an accident.''

Derek shrugged. ''Mama didn't think I was sufficiently apologetic about the whole thing.''

Lani felt laughter bubbling up at the thought of the large man before her being bullied by his mother. ''That's all right.'' Her voice was musical with the laughter she tried to suppress.

''I was hoping you'd let me take you out for dinner tonight. To kind of make up for it.'' Derek could hardly believe what he heard coming out of his mouth. He sounded like a high school kid asking the most popular girl in school to go out. Nervous city!

Lani considered the dinner invitation, ready with a firm no. Why get involved with a high-profile celebrity like Derek? She barely had time to breathe these days; a man as handsome and famous as Derek was bound to have a monstrous ego that was sure to demand too much of her precious personal time. But a polite yes tumbled from her lips instead. Her conscious mind seemed to have been overruled by her subconscious, and her subconscious apparently wanted to see Derek Wolfe again.

She agreed to meet him at The Lone Wolf that evening, then chased him out of the office so she could make her phone calls. If only it was as easy to chase him from her mind.

Pulsing with curiosity, Lani approached The Lone Wolf Bar and Grill that evening. Derek Wolfe's restaurant and sports bar had only been open for two months, but it had received a great deal of coverage in the local press. Her trepidation at being on a date with Derek was tempered by her desire to see the new ''in'' place to eat.

Derek met her outside and escorted her in, past the long line waiting for admittance. Lani noted the wide-eyed looks she received from the waiting patrons, the whispers speculating on her identity.

Lani had thought herself above such frivolity, but she had to admit to a little thrill of pleasure at the envious looks thrown her way. She felt like a celebrity herself as she accompanied the handsome former football star into the building.

The Lone Wolf enjoyed a prime location, situated right on the waterfront in downtown Lahaina. The lower level housed the bar, a beautiful thing made of *koa* that gleamed gold and brown in the evening light. A stylistic representation of Maui lassoing the moon was carved into the front of it. A wide-screen television high above the bar was showing a football game. Sports memorabilia—trophies, jerseys, and autographed balls—decorated the walls.

Lani approached the bar and ran her hand over the smooth golden wood. ''This is beautiful—a work of art.''

''I wish I could take credit for it, but it was already here when I bought the place. It was a failed nightclub,'' he explained. ''The owner spent too much setting up—the bank repossessed the place. That piece of wood probably represented a lot of the overspending, too. But it worked out for me. It was exactly what I wanted.''

He led her through the row of glass sliding doors that created the far wall, now open to allow entry of the cool sea breezes. Here a deck stretched out over the water at high tide. Round tables filled the area, which was about as large as the space indoors. Potted bougainvilleas placed around the rails provided splashes of brilliant color. Although it was still early, all of the tables were filled, and waiters and waitresses wearing T-shirts emblazoned with the Lone Wolf logo hurried to and fro.

''We serve sandwiches and snacks down here,'' Derek told her. ''The real restaurant is upstairs.''

Lani glanced around her. ''This is great, Derek. No wonder you're successful.'' She turned her eyes back to him. "But I'm starving—and you did invite me for dinner . . ."

Derek laughed. "No subtlety from you, I see." He took her arm and steered her back inside, to a staircase she'd barely noticed at the far end of the room. "I've reserved a table for us upstairs."

Above the bar was another room—twice its size. This room extended out toward the water, forming the roof of the lower patio. It too was decorated with various types of sports trophies and paraphernalia, but there were no television screens. Obviously the classier dining area, Lani thought with a smile. Like the deck below, it was filled to capacity.

Derek led her through the tables to a prime spot in the corner. The round table was slightly away from the others and looked out over the ocean, which was turning amazing colors of peach, pink, and purple as the sun set.

Lani found herself charmed by the man beside her as they worked their way through appetizers, dinner, and dessert. Although she'd been nervous in his presence at first, it had been a long time since that peanut butter sandwich. By the time they sat together over coffee, she felt stuffed with the delicious food, and warmly fuzzy from the excellent wine.

Derek leaned back in his chair, stretching his legs out before him. He looked relaxed and content as he drank his coffee. Lani had to admit to the same feelings herself.

Derek's next words broke the spell.

"I wanted to talk to you about Mama."

"What about her?" Lani, her mind still foggy from the warmth of the crowded room and the unaccustomed wine, looked at him blankly. "I don't really know your mother."

"No. But you have a mother yourself, I take it?"

He smiled at the joke, and Lani was embarrassed by a twittery giggle that escaped from her lips. Did that really come from her? She wished she wasn't so tired.

She became serious as she searched for an answer to his question. What was his question? Oh, yes. Mothers.

"Of course," she said. "Everyone has a mother."

Derek frowned. Why was she making it so difficult? It was hard for him to speak out about this, but he wanted to get a woman's opinion. And he didn't want to bother his sister

Tracey—she was the cause of most of this any-way.

"What I meant was, could you give me some insight as to what might be going on with Mama? You know—a female perspective?"

Lani thought it over. She hardly ever drank, but he'd ordered wine with dinner without even asking her preference. It seemed so so-phisticated to sip it, and it had a lovely fruity taste. But the glass always seemed to be full, so she wasn't sure how much she'd had.

Lani was finding it very difficult to think. And, although a breeze still blew through the open windows, it was beginning to feel ex-traordinarily warm in the restaurant.

She'd gotten up early, after only five hours of sleep, then had an extremely full day. Her eyelids were so heavy, she found herself strug-gling to keep them open.

Derek caught her as she began to slide over in her chair.

Chapter Three

With quiet efficiency, Derek caught Lani's slumping body, pulling her up against his side. Then, supporting most of her weight, and praying that his unpredictable knees would hold up, he led her to his office, conveniently close by. With any luck, no one in the busy dining room noticed that the woman he walked out with was not moving under her own power.

Derek's office was small and strictly utilitarian. Looking around quickly, he decided to put her in his chair behind the desk. It was the most comfortable one in the room. Arranging her in the large leather chair, he called to a passing waitress for a pot of strong coffee.

Doctor Kalima obviously wasn't used to drinking. What was he supposed to do now? He ran his hand through his hair, throwing the pale ginger waves into casual disorder. He shoved his hands into his pants pockets and paced up and down several times in the confined space. On his third trip past the desk, his left knee buckled. He stopped immediately, leaning against the solid bulk of the large desk for a moment, cursing his unreliable body.

As he stood there resting his knee, he looked across the desk at Lani. Her face was calm and peaceful—she looked as if she'd just closed her eyes for a brief nap. Would she accuse him of trying to make her drunk, or of drugging her? His first impression was that she wouldn't, but he didn't know her very well. And he did know that first impressions were not always accurate.

Checking first to be sure his knee would accept his full weight, he moved to the doorway and looked down the hall toward the kitchen. Where was that coffee? Not seeing any sign of Diane, the waitress he'd asked to get it, he resumed his pacing. He knew he should sit instead, but he refused to give up his favorite

way of thinking just because his knees sometimes caused problems.

He strode to the end of the room, executed
a sharp turn, and covered the distance back to
the door in half a minute. It had never occurred
to him that wine with their dinner would put
Lani to sleep. At least, he hoped she was just
asleep.

He rushed back to the chair behind the desk.
She looked like a sleeping person. Her
breathing was slow and easy. Derek found his
eyes wandering over her lovely face. Her thick
lashes made dark half-moons against slightly
flushed cheeks.

Flushed. Should her cheeks be flushed? He
put his hand on her forehead. Was it hot? He
really didn't know.

Up until a few minutes ago, when he'd
broached the topic of Mama, she'd been just
fine, chatting like any normal, sober person.
She seemed to be enjoying their dinner, the
wine, the conversation.

He moved away from Lani when Diane entered the room with a large pot of coffee and
two cups.

''Thanks, Diane.'' He looked between the
two women. ''Does she look ill?'' The concern

in his voice drew a surprised look from Diane. But he knew she had a teenage daughter and was sure to know more about fevers than he did.

Diane set her tray down on his desk and moved around it to look closely at Lani. "She looks okay to me. She's probably just sleeping. Look at those circles under her eyes. Maybe you should let her sleep."

Diane's remarks made him feel better, but he poured out a cup of coffee anyway. The sooner he got some into her the sooner she'd revive.

Visions of tabloid headlines still haunted him. Luckily he didn't even have a couch in his office. But if she wanted to run to the tabloids with it, the story could be made to look bad enough just as it was. She didn't seem like the tabloid type, but he'd learned that you could never tell from appearances. He hoped she really was the sensible, professional woman she appeared to be, but he didn't know her well enough to be sure. He'd enjoyed their time together—more than he cared to admit.

An hour later, after several cups of strong black coffee, Derek escorted Lani down the back stairs and out to the street.

''Where's your car parked? I'll drive you home.''

''You can't do that.''

''Sure I can. You're in no condition to drive anywhere.''

Although she was now awake, Lani still seemed to be thinking in slow motion. She struggled for what she knew was a logical reason behind her refusal. Her jumbled brain finally brought it forth. ''How will you get back?''

''Don't worry about it.''

They'd reached her car and she relinquished her keys.

''I've got a cell phone and I'll call Sal at the Grill here with directions. He'll come out and pick me up.''

He helped her settle into the passenger seat and moved around to the driver's side. Once he'd adjusted the seat to his greater height he started the engine and looked over at her expectantly.

Lani stared back at him. Her large dark eyes sparkled with the reflected light of the street lamps. More than ever, she resembled a porcelain doll, delicate and beautiful. A sharp desire to protect this lovely woman speared him with an intensity that left him breathless.

Derek was finding it difficult to concentrate. But he did need to know where she lived if he planned to take her home. "Well?"

She continued to stare at him in silence. He hoped she wasn't going to fall asleep again, at least not before she had time to tell him where she lived.

Then, before he could ask her again, she leaned forward and brushed a lock of hair from his brow. "You're such a handsome man, Derek."

Her breath fanned across his cheek as she spoke, fragrant with the coffee she'd consumed, warm from the heat of her body. A tightness gathered inside him as he fought to retain control. She had such appealing cherry red lips, and she seemed to be leaning ever closer to him. Was she going to kiss him?

But, inches from his lips, she stopped, unable to reach any farther without undoing her seat belt and shoulder harness. Thank goodness that was a task she wasn't likely to attempt at the moment. He hoped!

Derek leaned back as far from her as he could in the compact car and opened the window, taking in huge breaths of the cool, briny evening air.

Finally he turned back to his passenger. She was still facing him, watching him with half-closed eyes, a dreamy smile on her parted lips. He had to swallow hard before he could speak.

''Where do you live, Lani? Can you direct me to your place?''

''Sure. I live with Uncle Charles.''

''Uncle Charles,'' Derek repeated. He smiled. ''Mama calls him Charlie, but Charles suits him.''

His eyes moved over her face once again. She was still staring at him, a pleasant smile on her lips. He wondered if she was fully awake. ''So . . . Where does Uncle Charles live?''

Her voice was low and slow, as though she were speaking in a dream, but she managed to provide enough directions to guide him to her home.

By the time he pulled into the graveled drive, she was asleep once more. He took her into his arms. It would be easier to carry her inside than to attempt waking her again.

Light shone through the front windows and

a yellow "bug light" on the porch was on, so Derek rang the bell.

Charles Wong opened the door, a look of concern quickly washing over his features when he saw Derek's burden.

Derek explained about the wine he'd ordered with dinner and Lani's reaction to it while Charles directed him to her room. Together they placed her on the bed, removed her shoes, then pulled a quilt over her still-dressed figure.

Charles Wong was such a stately, old-fashioned-looking gentleman that Derek found himself unexpectedly embarrassed by the situation. He felt he owed the older man more of an explanation—and an apology, for bringing his niece home in such a state.

To his surprise, Charles forestalled him by offering him a drink. "Fruit juice," Charles hastily added.

"Thank you." Derek seated himself in the small but tasteful living room and accepted the glass of pineapple-orange juice that Charles soon provided.

"I want to apologize." Derek gave a short laugh, shaking his head as he thought of how his circumstances had changed. "It seems to be all I'm doing today."

He took a sip of his juice. The cold liquid was refreshing, and soothed his dry throat. He felt like a teenager again, facing the father of his date on their first evening together. And feeling guilty about it! About something that had been, after all, beyond his control.

"I feel real bad about bringing Lani home like this. But I assure you I had no idea she would react that way to the wine. We just had it with our dinner."

"I accept your apology."

Derek was impressed with the other man's grave nod, his formal acceptance of the apology. With his straight posture, well-cut white hair, and neat, pressed appearance, he could be a nineteenth-century gentleman.

Charles went on. "Lani rarely drinks anything stronger than fruit juice. She would not be used to wine, even with a meal. And she was especially tired today, I think."

"She did say something about a late night and an early start this morning." Derek shifted on the sofa, wondering where to take the conversation from here. He wanted to get away from apologies.

"Mama told me she enjoyed talking to you on the plane yesterday. She's always been nervous about flying, so I'm glad she had you to visit with and keep her distracted.''

''Yes, she did mention that.''

Derek took another sip with an inward sigh. Charles was a man of few words. But Sal still hadn't arrived, and he hadn't been able to ask Lani about his mother. Maybe Charles could offer some advice. He and Mama were of the same generation.

''Do you mind if I ask you a question?''

Charles indicated with a gesture that he could go ahead.

Derek took another sip of his drink, trying to organize his thoughts. His concerns about Mama were difficult to verbalize.

''Mama's always been a quiet person.''

Now that he'd started, Derek felt absurd asking a complete stranger for advice on his mother. Still, she was driving him crazy, and he felt helpless to explain what had gotten into her.

He took another sip of his drink and plunged on. ''At least I thought she was—quiet, that is. When we kids were young she stayed at home; she did a lot of cooking and sewed clothes for my sister and herself. She made curtains and pillows for the sofa. She certainly seemed happy.''

He put the almost empty juice glass down on the table, careful to place it on a coaster that Charles had provided. ''Then my father died a year and a half ago—and suddenly I don't even know her. Even physically I hardly recognize her; she has a new hairdo and new clothes.''

He ran his fingers through his hair and re-sisted an urge to get up and pace the small room. ''Just this morning she called me at the restaurant to say she's decided to take up ten-nis.'' He shook his head. ''She's never done anything athletic before. Ever.''

Charles smiled. ''She called me too. I'd told her I've started playing again recently. Hadn't played since I was a boy. I'd like to play with her sometime.'' Charles looked at the younger man. ''If you don't mind.''

Derek looked at the older man, trying to hide his surprise. Charles was asking his permission to play tennis with his mother. Maybe even to court her. The old-fashioned word came easily to Derek's mind in reference to Charles Wong.

Stifling a sudden impulse to laugh at what struck him as a reversal of roles, Derek stood and put out his hand. "Dr. Wong, it's a pleasure to know you. I'm sure you and Mama will have some good matches."

Imbued with old-fashioned manners, Charles stood as soon as Derek did. He took his hand gladly, a smile spreading over his face. "Please. Call me Charles."

Before anything more could be said, the sound of a car on the gravel drive broke the quiet of the night.

Derek glanced at the front window. "That'll be my ride. Thanks for the drink." With a final nod, he was gone.

Derek didn't realize until he got home that Charles had never really commented about Mama and her changing attitudes. All he'd done was provide the answer to Mama's sudden interest in tennis.

Lani slipped two Tylenol tablets into her mouth and sipped from a bottle of water. Thankfully, Saturday was a short day at the office. She'd had mostly well-baby visits this morning, from working mothers who could only come in on the weekends. She loved the well-baby visits, though the babies weren't always as happy to see her.

She rubbed at her aching head as she sorted out the messages on her desk in preparation for making the day's allotment of phone calls. It would be a long time before she enjoyed a glass of wine with her dinner again. Bright color suffused her face as she thought of collapsing that way on Derek Wolfe. On Derek Wolfe! In the most chic restaurant in Lahaina! It was mortifying.

She checked her watch as she reached for the phone, wondering how long it would take before the Tylenol took effect. But before her hand closed over the receiver, the phone rang. Startling her as it did, she didn't manage to pick it up until after the second ring.

"Dr. Kalima." She used her best professional voice, proud that she was able to function well even when she was tired and headachy.

"Hello, Lani. How are you this morning?"

The rich, mellow tones of Derek's voice were instantly recognizable. She sat upright in her chair, dark red flaming her cheeks as she remembered the previous evening. It had to be the most humiliating experience of her life, falling asleep at the table after a glass or two of wine!

"I'm fine, thank you," she finally replied.

"I hoped there were no lingering aftereffects."

Uncertain what to say to this, Lani remained silent.

Derek's next comment filled the awkward pause. "And I wanted to apologize."

"Apologize?" Lani was so surprised her voice came out in a squeak. So much for her professionalism.

"Yeah. I should have watched your wine comsumption more carefully. I should have realized you weren't a drinker. Next time I'll know better."

Anger rushed through her as she gripped the phone furiously. But her voice was deceptively calm when she spoke. "You mean it was all your fault that I had too much to drink last night and fell asleep at the table?"

"Yeah."

Derek's voice sounded relieved. He must have thought she'd be upset with him over the incident and this was his way of taking responsibility. What a macho jerk!

"Well, Mr. Wolfe." Lani began in a calm, collected manner, but her words grew more rapid and emotion-charged as she spoke.

''Thank you very much for your call. But I am just fine. I can take responsibility for my own behavior, thank you very much. It's my own fault that I had too much wine. I should have known better. Thank you for your call.''

And she slammed the receiver back into its cradle.

Before he could decide to call back, she picked it up again and began to dial.

Derek heard the loud click followed by a dial tone and blinked at the phone in surprise. What was wrong with her? He was just trying to do the right thing. . . . He'd never apologized so much in his whole life as he had in the past three days, and most of the apologies were directed her way. And this was the thanks he got.

But there was no time to worry about that now. His mother had opened the study door and was striding into the room. He recognized that look. She wore it often lately. Just what he needed!

He came around the desk, seating himself beside her on the sofa. Mama smiled at him, but he found it hard to relax. For one thing, she was dressed in a short little pleated skirt, a T-shirt, and bright white sneakers. Did all fifty-somethings play tennis in those tiny little skirts?

"So how was the first tennis lesson?"

"Good." She rearranged herself against the pillows, pulling the little skirt downward. It didn't help much. She still showed a good deal of chubby thigh. "I enjoyed it. The instructor said I'm a natural." She smiled proudly.

"Did you know Charles Wong plays?"

"Oh? Does he?" All innocence, Barbara smiled at her son.

Derek knew that look. He'd done it himself as a child too many times not to know she was pretending not to know something she knew perfectly well.

"Maybe you two can play together sometime. I understand he's cutting back on his work hours now that Lani has joined the practice."

Mama's eyes examined his face with interest. "How was your date with her last night?"

"Good." Best to be noncommittal. If he wasn't careful, she'd have him engaged before he knew it. Literally.

Barbara gave him a knowing look but apparently decided to humor him. She changed the subject. "Derek, I'd like your advice about buying a new car."

Derek was surprised. "Of course, Mama. Is something wrong with the car you have?" He'd gotten her a nice Buick sedan when she'd joined him on Maui six months ago.

"Nothing's wrong with it." She paused a moment to cross her legs, then raised her eyes to her son's. There was a defensive look about her. Or was it defiant? "I want a sports car. And I need some advice about prices and types," she added.

Derek was stunned. First the hair and the clothes. Then the tennis lessons. Now a sports car! What had happened to the quiet, old-fashioned mother he remembered?

"A sports car." He stood and paced toward the desk and back. "Are you sure?"

Barbara nodded. "I thought a convertible. So I can drive with the top down and enjoy the nice weather we have here."

Derek nodded, still staring at her as though she was a stranger. "How much do you want to spend?" Although she lived with him and he covered all the household expenses, Barbara had an independent income from his father's pension and insurance.

Barbara shifted again, this time facing him with an earnest expression on her face. "I wanted you to advise me about that too. If you would."

Derek looked at his mother. She had a pleading look centered on him. What could he do?

"Of course I'll help you, Mama."

Chapter Four

Lani glanced at her watch as she wheeled the grocery cart around the corner. Respiratory ailments were still rampant among Maui's youngest inhabitants, and as a result, she'd been running late all day. But if she could get the paper towels she needed and get out of the store in the next fifteen minutes, she'd have enough time to pick up her nephew's birthday present before the gift shop closed.

If only Uncle Charles was attending the party with her, then all this scramble would be unnecessary. But he was the guest of honor at a banquet tomorrow evening, where he would receive a Good Samaritan award for his work in saving the lives of two small children and their parents after a serious traffic accident several months ago. The past week had been so busy, Lani had never bothered with a major trip to the supermarket to restock the kitchen. She wanted to do that now before she left for the weekend, so that Uncle Charles would be able to manage with the least amount of trouble. He was doing so much to help her establish her career, she felt that keeping up the house and kitchen was the least she could do.

Hurrying down the aisle, she snatched a box of crackers from the shelf, hardly breaking her fast-paced stride. Then she flew around the next corner praying it held the paper goods.

And crashed into another cart!

"Oh, no! I'm so sorry! I . . ."

Lani was babbling so fast, she hadn't even looked at the person pushing the other cart. Her eyes finally moved beyond the disheveled groceries in both carts to the dark pleated slacks and neat aloha shirt behind it; upward to the large broad chest covered with a conservative Hawaiian print in blues and grays; then still upward, to the face above the athletic masculine body. . . .

"Oh, my gosh," she cried. She was staring

into smoky blue eyes in a handsome, tanned face. And the laugh lines around his eyes and mouth were already creasing.

''You!'' The exclamation came from both simultaneously. But Derek said it with a smile, Lani with a trace of alarm.

Derek was checking out the two carts, as well as Lani's trim figure. There was obvious amusement in his voice as he concluded, ''Well, nothing seems to be injured.''

''N-no.'' Lani was flustered. She hadn't seen Derek since their disastrous dinner date a week ago. Who would have guessed she'd run into him here?

Before she realized what she was about to do, she blurted out her thought. ''I never expected to see you in a *grocery* store.'' Then, embarrassed by the blunt statement, she felt color flooding her cheeks.

But Derek's smile just widened. ''A guy's got to eat.''

Lani felt sure her face must be as red as that of the sunburned tourist pushing her cart around them. She hoped an explanation would redeem her. ''I guess I thought that Barbara would handle it, or that you'd have a cook.''

''I do. Have a cook, I mean. But she's on

Lanai right now, visiting her family. Her father's been sick. As for Mama, when she moved in with me she declared herself retired from all cooking." He shook his head, obviously baffled by this announcement from his mother. "When she heard we'd be without Luana for a week, she decided to go on a diet. She's eaten nothing but raw vegetables for the past three days. So I'm on my own."

"Don't you eat at the restaurant?" Honest curiosity was visible in her eyes.

"Sometimes. It's not open for breakfast though."

"Oh." She felt tongue-tied and juvenile. She should have known that.

Derek gave her a stern look though mischief danced in his blue-gray eyes.

"And I *can* cook," he informed her. "I'm surprised at you, Dr. Kalima," he went on, with mock severity. "It's really very sexist of you, implying that I can't prepare a meal for myself and Mama—or shop for the supplies needed."

Obviously distressed at his teasing accusation, Lani rushed into speech. "It isn't that I assumed you couldn't cook. It's just that I guess I thought celebrities like yourself would have a cook. . . .'' Finding herself floundering in a sea of grammatical errors, Lani let her voice trail off. She was an intelligent woman of thirty, yet whenever she was around this man she reverted to adolescence. What was the matter with her?

Derek, thank goodness, didn't seem to notice. He looked beyond the carts to the end-cap display, a huge mound of red-and-white cans. ''Good thing we didn't topple the display,'' he said, reaching out to pick up a can of soup.

Lani agreed.

''So.'' Derek glanced down at the label of the can in his hand and smiled at her. ''Do you think I need some cream of mushroom soup?''

Lani had to smile back. ''Not for breakfast.'' Her arm stretched out beyond him for a can from another part of the display. ''Now, tomato, that's a more versatile soup. You can eat that anytime, don't you think?''

Derek took the can from her hand, his fingers brushing hers in the process. Warmth radiated up to her wrist and she quickly pulled away. Blinking in confusion at the curious effect this man seemed to have on her, she clutched at several of the cans in the display, adding mushroom and cream of chicken soup to the accumulation in her cart.

Derek put the can of tomato soup alongside his other purchases, then picked up the mushroom again. "Actually, cream of mushroom soup does have possibilities for breakfast. For gravy, over biscuits, in a kind of Southern-style breakfast."

"Obviously you're a more creative cook than I am." Lani, who preferred fruit and toast first thing in the morning, tried not to think about his high-calorie, fat-laden possibilities.

"Do you have any plans for the weekend?"

Surprised at the non sequitur, Lani turned back to him, wide-eyed. She found him gazing at her, his look oddly intense. Could Derek Wolfe really care what she was doing this weekend?

"Yes, I do. It's my weekend off and I'm driving out to Hana to visit my parents. And my nephew is having his first birthday luau." She glanced at her watch. "Oh, no. I'm really late now."

"You aren't going to drive out tonight, are you?"

Lani responded to the concern in his voice.

Obviously, he was familiar with the long, winding road, not the best place to be at night.

"No. But I have a lot to do before I leave. Most important, I have to pick up Keoki's birthday gift. From a shop that will be closing in about fifteen minutes."

She pulled her cart away from his and turned it toward the checkout, rushing once again. They'd have to manage without paper towels until she could get back to the store.

"Give my best to Barbara."

Lani called the comment over her shoulder, meaning it as a good-bye, but Derek pushed his cart along beside hers, easily matching her stride with his longer legs.

"I will. But I think your Uncle Charles sees more of her than I do."

"I didn't know that." Lani had started to empty her cart onto the counter, but paused a moment to consider Derek's last statement. She remembered how happy Charles and Barbara had appeared when they were together that day at the airport. Uncle Charles *had* been looking better, more relaxed, lately. Maybe Barbara Wolfe was the reason, not the outdoor recreation he was suddenly indulging in.

As she went back to emptying her cart, Lani

heard Derek clear his throat to gain her attention. She turned to face him. "Yes?"

"Why don't you let me drive you to Hana?"

Lani stopped, her hand, holding a carton of orange juice, suspended over the counter. Derek watched the play of emotions on her face. He knew he affected her, just as she did him.

"Why would you do that?"

Derek thought quickly. "A friend of mine on the mainland is thinking of buying a place out there. He asked me about it, but I haven't been out that way since a visit several years ago." It wasn't precisely a lie. A former colleague of his *was* planning to buy a house in Hana when he retired next year. And he had asked him about the island.

He watched Lani place the orange juice on the counter and reach for the last of the items in the cart.

"Don't you have to be at the restaurant over the weekend?" Lani pulled the cart through and stepped up to the counter, but she was still facing behind her, looking at Derek. "Saturday and Sunday must be your busiest days."

Derek nodded. "I've been training an assistant. It's the only way I'll ever be able to take time off, and I wanted to take Mama to the Big

Island to see the volcano the next time it erupts. This would be a good way to see how he handles the place on his own.''

Derek paused while Lani wrote out her check. Luckily the store was shorthanded tonight, so he had a few more minutes while the checker bagged the groceries.

''I hope you don't take this the wrong way, but you look very tired.'' He frowned as she handed the check to the cashier. ''Not that you don't look lovely,'' he added, ''but you do look tired.''

Lani shrugged. She *was* tired. It had been an awful week at work. Dozens of children arrived with colds and flu, plus all the usual well-baby visits, ear infections, and assorted cuts and bruises that parents worried over. Then there were the trips back and forth to the hospital in Wailuku. . . .

She didn't look at Derek but she couldn't help but be aware of his presence beside her as he finished unloading his cart. His offer was so tempting. The busy week had left her exhausted. She wanted nothing more than to spend the whole weekend at home, catching up on her sleep.

But going home, home to Hana, was always

a wonderful pickup. And this weekend, there was little Keoki's first birthday luau. She would never miss such an important family occassion, so it would be wonderful to have someone else tackle the long drive.

She paused. But of course if he drove her out, she'd have to offer him a place to stay Saturday night. After the long morning drive and the afternoon party—which was sure to stretch out into the night—it would be much too late to start back.

She swallowed. Her parents had plenty of room. They would be glad to have him. Why not accept his offer? It would be better than starting out on the long, narrow highway in her exhausted condition, chancing an accident because she was still embarrassed about last week's dinner.

As Lani turned to Derek and accepted, she felt a little thrill of pleasure. Or was it just the supercooled air in the grocery store causing a chill to pass through her lightly clad body?

Chapter Five

The drive began quietly, and very early the next morning. With the sun just lightening the eastern sky, they were both a little sleepy, both a little embarrassed—Derek at so brashly proposing that he drive and in effect inviting himself to her family party; Lani because she still remembered her humiliating slumping act at his dinner table, and all the other less than flattering meetings she'd had with him. From their collision at the airport to their crash at the grocery store, the only "normal" time they'd spent together was in her office during his visit with Justin.

Their initial conversation was formal and

stilted, of the did-you-sleep-well and nice-morning-for-a-drive variety. Lani complimented Derek on his comfortable car, then the small talk dissolved into quiet.

Derek hid his surprise at his first sight of Lani. She was casually dressed in faded, worn jeans and a baggy T-shirt. She looked impossibly young and prettier than ever.

Derek realized that this was the first time he'd seen Lani when she wasn't dressed for work. The conservative suits and the skirts and blouses he'd seen her wearing up to now were obviously her professional clothes.

So was this the real Lani, he wondered?

As they moved along the highway, Lani turned her eyes to the pineapple fields outside, following the dark green rows up to the green mountain beyond. Morning comes quickly in the subtropics and it was already bright, the sun shining through spotty clouds moving quickly across the sky.

"It's nice to be back." She sighed with pleasure at the familiar sights of her native island, speaking more to herself than to her companion. Her voice trailed off as she thought of the years she'd spent at various schools and hospitals in California. They'd been good years for the most part. But it was hard to believe she'd ever contemplated staying in California to practice. She'd missed Maui. Now more than ever she realized how much. No matter how maudlin it sounded, it was good to be back.

Derek seemed to understand. ''I know just what you mean. I've lived here full-time for less than a year, but already I can't imagine leaving. Permanently, that is. I can hardly believe I considered staying in Dallas.''

Lani was still staring out the window, but now she turned. ''Did you? Consider settling in Dallas, I mean. You're not from there, are you?''

''No, I'm from Indiana, but I did consider staying in Dallas. I lived there for almost ten years while I was playing for the Mustangs.'' One side of his mouth pulled down in a frown as he thought of something. ''In fact, I often remember that bar in Dallas fondly, when Mama is telling me about her new exploits.''

Exploits. Lani considered his choice of words.

''She bought a fancy sports car, you know.''

Lani laughed. ''Yes. I saw it. She drove over to show it off to Uncle Charles.'' Lani exam-

ined Derek's profile. "Surely you don't be-
grudge her spending money on herself. She
was so happy about the car. She reminded me
of a child on Christmas morning."

"No. I've got lots of money. Besides, Mama
used her own money to buy the car."

Lani swallowed hard at his offhand remark
about his personal finances. People who had
money didn't think about it very much. No, it
was people like herself, who desperately
needed it, who thought about money all the
time.

Most people thought doctors made huge
amounts of money—her old school friends did.
Whenever she ran into one of them, someone
was sure to call her "a rich doctor now." But
for new physicians like herself the reality was
far different. For one thing, it would take years
to get out from under the load of debt she'd
incurred paying for her education. And the average person didn't realize how much insurance costs cut into a doctor's income.

Lani's face underwent a variety of expressions as she struggled with thoughts of finances
and how they affected her life. Soon she would
settle into a routine of practice and she
wouldn't always feel so tired. At least she

hoped it would work that way. But until she could do something about her monstrous debts, how could she fulfill that largest of all dreams—having a family of her own? A family *and* a career—to Lani that would be the ideal life.

Derek's voice brought her back to the present as he continued his conversation.

"Mama doesn't really have to live with me. My father was a saver and he left her comfortably off."

Derek, his eyes on the road, didn't notice Lani's changing expressions as she worked through her inexorable concerns. His mind was still occupied with thoughts of his mother. Maybe now would be the time to discuss her with Lani. It was what he'd hoped to do a week ago at their fateful dinner date. And they still had over two hours of driving before them.

He sighed, overwhelmed by memories of earlier days. "My father died shortly before my knees gave out and I had to retire from football."

Lani's tender heart went out to him as she heard the sad acceptance in his voice. She wondered how long it had taken before he could speak about his physical weakness in such even tones.

"So when I made the decision to retire here, I told Mama she was welcome to come and stay with me." He paused a minute while increased traffic took his attention. "If I'd only known."

Lani caught the subtle plea in his tone, but knew there was little she could say. He obviously needed to talk to someone about his problems with his mother and it looked like she'd been elected.

Lani immediately scolded herself for being so insensitive. Doctors were supposed to care about people and she could tell that Derek was honestly confused and worried. If she could help, she would and gladly—especially since she was growing fond of Barbara. She just wished being with Derek didn't leave her so confused.

Derek began by telling Lani something about his childhood. "Mama was a holdover. While most of my friends' moms worked, she was a stay-at-home mom like those mothers in the 1950s sitcoms. She packed us nutritious lunches and was always there when we got home from school. She sewed drapes for the house and frilly dresses for my sister Tracey. She made wonderful Halloween costumes for us. And she was always cooking—good hearty meals, breads, biscuits, cookies, pies. . . . You should have seen the cake she made for my ninth birthday.''

Derek's fond look as he remembered the cake changed and he shook his head in dismay. ''I was flabbergasted when she said she'd retired from cooking. I'd always thought it was her favorite thing to do. Now she says she would have liked to work outside the house, in a department store, but Dad was the traditional type and didn't want her to.''

''So she gave up her own career plans for him.'' Lani's voice was quiet. She was getting a whole different perspective on Barbara. ''She must have really loved your father.''

Derek shrugged. ''Kids, especially boys, don't notice stuff like that. But now, looking back, I'm sure they had something pretty special between them. But then too, Dad had a very strong, dominant personality.''

''Why does it not surprise me to hear that?'' Lani murmured under her breath.

If Derek heard her, he made no indication. They were approaching a one-lane bridge, and

Derek had to pull over to allow a pickup truck coming from the other direction to proceed. Once the other driver had passed, waving a *shaka* sign in thanks, Derek drove back onto the road and continued on his way. He especially appreciated the local driver's gesture. Although new to the island, he had quickly learned it meant "take it easy" and was a way of showing thanks and goodwill. But even as he smiled at the young man in the truck, the major portion of his mind was still mulling over his newly complex understanding of his mother's personality.

"So you think she was being repressed all those years and now suddenly she's having another adolesence or something?" he asked.

"Maybe. Just what exactly has she done besides retire her pots and pans?" Lani wondered if Barbara had just decided to retire, period. After all, men got to retire at a certain age. But all Barbara had ever done was cook and keep house. Derek was sure to have someone in to do the cleaning; giving up the cooking may have been her way of liberating herself, her way of "retiring."

Lani shook her head, sending her long hair back over her shoulders and away from her face. She would never be able to give up her career for a man, no matter how much she loved him. Being a doctor was too much a part of her character to be so easily discarded. With a somber expression, she turned her attention back to Derek, who was answering her question.

"Right after Dad died, she didn't do anything. Just stayed around the house. Tracey and I were beginning to worry about her, in fact. Then, after a couple of months, she started going out again—you know, church, her women's club. That kind of thing."

He paused for a moment, remembering that worrisome time. "Dad died in the spring and that Christmas we all went to Tracey's house for the holiday. Tracey had a new baby and it was easier to go there. I was out, injured, and managed to get over for a couple of days. Mama met my plane at the airport on Christmas Eve—and I didn't even recognize her!"

Lani turned to watch him, her eyebrows raised in surprise. "What happened?"

"She'd been at Tracey's for a couple of weeks already. Seems they'd gone shopping. Tracey convinced her she needed a new wardrobe. Updated, I think they called it. Tracey said it was just what Mama needed to pull her out of her funk.''

Lani could tell from the tone of his voice that all this female business was more than any sane male could comprehend.

''So Mama apparently donated all her comfortable old pantsuits to the Salvation Army and bought new pants and skirts and tops. Co-ordinated, Tracey called them. Then, because she had all these nice stylish clothes, Tracey told her she had to go get a new hairdo.''

Derek frowned at the thick vegetation lining both sides of the road. He didn't even see it. He was remembering Mama's beautiful hair. When he was a toddler he loved to sit and watch her brush it, a long gleaming swath of ginger brown that poured down her back and over her shoulders.

He blinked himself back into the present. ''Anyway, there went her beautiful long hair. She used to wear it up on top of her head. The gray went too, and it's too red now, though it's close to her natural color. Like I said—she met me at the airport on Christmas Eve and I didn't even recognize her.''

''It must have been quite a shock.''

''You better believe it.'' Derek still couldn't

get over the change in her appearance. "But that was just the beginning. I was already thinking about retiring and opening a restaurant. And as soon as I asked her to live with me, she went nuts."

"Nuts?"

"Yeah. She'd never interfered in my adult life until then. Suddenly she was everywhere."

Lani wanted to laugh, but managed to suppress the urge. She could see that Derek was very emotional about the whole subject of his mother. But she did find it somewhat funny— this great big grown man claiming his diminutive mother was trying to run his life.

"I told you I almost settled in Dallas. I'd made a lot of friends there over the years."

Lani sobered. He probably had a lot of female friends there too. But then a man like Derek Wolfe could easily make female friends anywhere.

"Mama was dead set against Dallas. Said she was too old to put up with that kind of weather. As soon as I mentioned looking at a place on Maui she started after me to get it."

"So the city of Lahaina has Barbara to thank for The Lone Wolf."

Derek shrugged. "I liked the facility here.

And I like Maui. I did take her feelings into account. But she didn't have to live with me either. As I said before, Dad left her comfortable. And I'll always help her out. She could have gotten a nice condo in Florida, or Arizona. She could have gotten her own place here, even if I had decided to stay on the mainland.''

Lani didn't know Barbara very well, but Derek's mother did strike her as a person who cared deeply for family. She was the type who needed someone to look after. When she lost her husband, she'd decided her son needed her. Derek might wonder, but Lani was sure Barbara would have lived in Dallas if Derek had remained there.

''Barbara likes to be needed. The only way you'll get her off your back is if she finds a new husband.''

Lani could tell by Derek's reaction that this had never occurred to him. Although he kept his eyes on the road, and his driving ability remained excellent, it was obvious to her that he was mulling over the idea of Barbara needing a husband.

Lani let him think, turning her attention to the old familiar landmarks beyond the window.

Quiet reigned, a calm, easy silence that felt right and comfortable.

As yet another lovely waterfall came into sight, she felt her eyelids drooping. Blinking her eyes back open, Lani continued to stare out the window. But it was so comfortable in Derek's car. So peaceful. So quiet.

Derek continued to think about Mama. He wondered why the idea of Mama remarrying hadn't occurred to him. Now that Lani had mentioned it, he realized she was right. It was just what Mama needed—someone to give her life meaning again. He wondered why Tracey hadn't thought of it.

Derek turned his head, ready to thank Lani for helping him sort out his problem.

One quick glance was enough. Lani sat, her neck cricked at an awkward angle, her lovely head turned toward the window, her beautiful, long dark hair spread out over her shoulder and chest.

Derek sighed. Lani Kalima was cutting his male ego down every time they were together. Used to being fawned over by eager females, Derek was finding himself at a loss in this situation. For Lani had fallen asleep on him. Again!

Chapter Six

Derek liked to drive. On the mainland, when the stress of a big game, or some personal problem bothered him, he would get into his car and take a long drive. He especially liked the thruways, for the long concrete ribbons allowed high speeds and low concentration.

Since moving to Maui though, the distances were so short, the longest trip he made these days was between Lahaina and the Kahului airport. He considered the thirty- to forty-minute drive a short hop, but he knew that native islanders thought it a fairly long drive.

Now he rediscovered the pleasure of driving as he traveled on the Hana Highway. The tall

71

green mountains, the blue ocean, the changing greens of the roadside vegetation . . . It was as different as could be from the mainland thruways. It was enough to bring back the pleasant feeling of inactivity he'd always relished while behind the wheel. The switchbacks, the one-lane bridges—they just made the trip more challenging and more enjoyable.

For most of the last ten years, Derek had been living life in the fast lane, first as a top college football star, then as a member of the popular Dallas Mustangs. Being a sports celebrity, and an extremely handsome one, had been his entrée into the fast-paced life of Dallas's highest society. At first it was heady—the small-town boy partying with the rich and famous, beautiful women on his arm for any occasion. Eventually, it had just been the way things were.

Finally, he'd become vaguely bored with it all. That, and the increasingly serious problems with his knees, had been behind the decision to retire and purchase a business.

At his arrival in Lahaina, he was immediately pulled into the frantic whirl of celebrity occasions in the tourist town. So far, he'd enjoyed the partying, and of course the publicity engendered by such activity was good for his restaurant. Business at The Lone Wolf was booming in the short time it had been open, and he wasn't too modest to admit that his name was the biggest draw.

But now, with Mama driving him crazy, and the new business running smoothly, he found himself once again getting restless. Urged by some of his buddies, he'd taken up golf. But although he enjoyed the time on the fairways, there was the constant worry on his part that his knees might not hold up through the entire eighteen holes. And he didn't want to ride a cart when the others were walking, thereby admitting his physical limitations. So the game hadn't gripped him the way it did some of his friends.

Now, on a narrow, winding road running along sunny white sand beaches and through green swaths of rain forest, he found the smooth rhythm of driving spread a calm through him that was both relaxing and enjoyable. He'd needed this. Whatever strange impulse had led him to offer his services as driver, this trip was turning out better than he'd ever expected. And he had a small island doctor to thank.

* * *

Lani awakened slowly. A softly sung country tune was playing. As the ballad drifted through her still sleepy brain, she remembered where she was. Sitting up in her seat quickly, surreptitiously stretching her cramped muscles, she fixed a penetrating look out the window, taking in their surroundings.

''Where are we?''

Derek laughed. He was feeling good. He was enjoying the ride, he'd enjoyed the earlier talk with Lani, and he was enjoying a favorite country music tape.

''I'm afraid to risk my pronunciation in front of a native.''

Lani had to smile too. She'd heard enough slaughtered Hawaiian over the years to appreciate his dilemma. ''Well, take a guess.''

''Way-na-papa,'' he guessed.

Lani laughed again. ''Good try.'' She peered out the windows. ''Waianapanapa,'' she added, pronouncing it slowly and drawing out the syllables so he could hear the proper way to say it.

''Why-ah-nah-pa-nah-pa,'' he repeated after her.

''Perfect.'' She grinned as she gave him the

compliment, then turned to continue gazing out the window. "We'll be there soon."

As the sky began to color with the approach of night, Derek sat back on the wide porch, his legs thrown out casually before him, a tall glass of pineapple-flavored iced tea in his hand.

What a great day it had been. Lani's brother Mark, father of the birthday boy, all her relatives and especially her parents, had welcomed him like a long-lost friend, assuring him that they were glad to have him and that there was plenty of room for him to stay the night. Lani was a charming hostess, introducing him to everyone, helping him choose food from the vast tables, making him feel comfortable.

The luau was set up in the large carport adjacent to the Kalimas' house. Across a wide-open, grassy field stood another, newer house where Lani's brother and his family lived. The party quickly overflowed into the wide lawn created by this field and onto the porches of the two homes.

The food was plentiful and filling. Of course there was *kalua* pig and sweet potatoes, *poi* and *lomi* salmon. But Derek found himself fascinated by some of the dishes Lani claimed were old family luau favorites. He, an up-and-coming restaurateur in the islands, thought he knew a lot about the local cuisine—and found he had much still to learn.

And all afternoon, he watched Lani's transformation. Either that short nap in the car had had great restorative properties, or there was some magic in the cool air at the Kalima ranch. For Lani's tiredness seemed to drop away like the bright yellow blossoms that drifted from the branches of the enormous shower tree that shaded the grassy lawn.

Now, as the sky grew darker, teenage boys were setting out torches, lighting a large area around the edge of the yard. Some of the guests were tuning up ukuleles and guitars, and several drums had appeared. It was time for the entertainment portion of the evening.

Derek looked over at the guest of honor. Little Keoki Kalima was cradled in his Auntie Lani's arms, deep in slumber, his thumb stuck in his mouth. His birthday outfit was smeared with chocolate from his cake and his chubby brown legs were dusty from playing in the open spaces between the houses. His chest rising and falling with each breath, his mouth quirking upward in a smile around his thumb, he was the picture of contentment.

Lani saw Derek looking over and smiled. She had the sweetest smile. He wished they were sitting together on the wooden glider at the opposite end of the porch. It would make the day perfect if he could sit here with her now, his arm around her, the baby asleep in her lap.

The pleasantness of such a domestic thought startled Derek and he took another long, hard look at Lani. Prettier than ever, she sat with her nephew, the gentle smile still on her lips. Her face radiated contentment and happiness. Was that what he found so appealing? For she was getting to him in a way never achieved by any of the tall, cool models he'd dated in the past.

The door to the house opened with a creak of old wood, and Lani's parents came out to join them. Cyrilla and Larry Kalima were obviously a happy and affectionate couple, arms entwined around each other's waists.

''Hello, Grandma. Grandpa.'' Lani smiled at her parents as she continued to rock in her chair, the abundant dark hair of her parents' only grandchild tickling the bottom of her chin with each forward movement.

Derek too offered a greeting as the couple sat down together in the wooden glider. Then he sighed in contentment.

"I guess you've heard it before, but this is a nice place you've got here."

Larry nodded. A big man—not more than six feet tall, but broad shouldered and muscular, he completely filled his half of the glider. "Yep. Mark and I are real lucky to have this place. We'll never be rich in money, but the land—now that's worth having."

Cyrilla nodded her reply. Her eyes roamed out across the beautiful landscape. "Yes. We're real lucky here." She sighed. "Sometimes I wish . . ."

Her voice trailed off as Lani's gaze turned her way.

"Don't start, Mom. You know I have to have my practice in a more populated area. I have all those loans to repay."

She said populated, but they knew she really meant affluent. In addition to the larger population in Lahaina, she received a lot of business from the hotels, who referred their guests with sick children to her. That and the referrals from

Uncle Charles were helping her establish herself quickly. Her practice was off to a good start and she couldn't give it all up to move back to the ranch, much as her parents would like to have her there.

Feeling some of the familial tension crackling in the cool evening air, Derek decided to change the subject.

"Do you ever feel isolated out here?" Derek thought it a beautiful place, but he saw it more as a hideaway. The former colleague he'd told Lani about was viewing it that way—a nice winter home away from it all. And while Derek could imagine buying a vacation home in Hana, he couldn't picture himself living so far from nowhere full-time.

"Not at all," Larry replied. "We have the family close by," he said, gesturing over to the house next door. "And there are all the *paniolos*. They all live within a few miles. We have good neighbors."

Cyrilla laughed. "Yes, it's just stores and theatres and restaurants that we're far from."

"Poor Mom." Lani joined her laughter.

Derek smiled too, to see the interaction among them all. He enjoyed family times like

this. Maybe he could have them again if Mama
would . . .

He moved his mind away from Mama and
focused on the music beginning in the yard.
The five of them sat on the porch for over an
hour as the light faded and the music floated
out around them. They weren't too far away to
see the performers as they took turns showing
off their hulas and other Polynesian dances.

Keoki's mother performed a lively Tahitian
number before coming over to retrieve the
birthday boy. But still, the others sat on. There
was a magic in the night that transcended understanding. Tonight was special. Derek was
uncertain what made it that way. He just knew
that he was not alone in sensing the charm of
the evening.

Lani looked across the darkened landscape,
able to discern the rough edges of the familiar
horizon. She missed the warm presence of her
nephew in her lap. And she was terribly aware
of Derek's large presence, even though they sat
several feet apart, in separate chairs. The large
wooden chairs stood there on the old porch,
side by side, not even touching. Yet Lani could
almost feel Derek beside her.

This night, this whole day actually, had been

special. From the long, quiet drive to the casual fun of her nephew's birthday luau, the day had been a huge success.

Now she stared unseeing at several of her young cousins, lined up and laughing as they danced to "One Paddle, Two Paddle." How could she be feeling this way about Derek, Lani wondered? True, he was a handsome, charismatic man. But she was a sane, sensible adult. And she didn't really know him at all.

Lani, like many other people, often scanned the headlines in the tabloids while she waited in the grocery checkout lines. And she'd seen his name in those screaming headlines too many times. His name was only vaguely familiar to her until he moved to Lahaina. But then it became more noticeable. He'd become a regular in the local paper as well—and every photo showed him with a beautiful woman on his arm. And though she knew better than to believe half of what the tabloids printed, what about the other half?

No, he wasn't her type.

Stifling an oversized yawn, Lani rose from her seat and walked over to her parents, still swinging quietly in the glider. "I'm enjoying this, but I'm pretty well wiped out. I'm going to go in to bed.''

With no self-consciousness, she bent to place a kiss on the cheek of each of her parents. They in turn returned her affectionate good night.

Lani then crossed the porch, stopping beside Derek's chair. ''Good night, Derek. Please stay and enjoy yourself. Come in anytime you're ready.''

Her hand drifted to his arm. The skin was warm, the texture slightly rough from a thin coating of dark hairs. Her voice was soft but clear in the cool night air.

''Thank you for the ride.'' Her eyes were dark pools in the moving light of the torches. ''It's been a lovely day, hasn't it?''

The smile that tilted her lips made Derek's heart flip over. There was something about her smile . . .

For hours after Lani disappeared indoors, Derek remained in the porch chair, quietly soaking in the peacefulness of the scene. How many years had it been since he'd participated in a big family party like this? Not since he was a boy back in Indiana.

He had to grin at the incongruous comparison. The flat plains of his native Hoosier state were entirely different from lush Maui with its huge mountain and verdant green valleys. And the kids who cluttered those old summer picnics he remembered were barefoot, clad in overalls and ripped blue jeans.

He gazed out over the grassy yard. There were kids aplenty here, even so late. Most of them were asleep on the laps of the adults, with toddlers sprawled across spreads of brightly colored patchwork squares. They were barefoot too, but there the comparison ended. These kids wore colorful baggy shorts and swimsuits, and many of the little girls wore bright ruffled muumuus.

Derek had expected the party to be pretty loud by now, since there was plenty of beer around, had been all afternoon. But the only rowdy bunch was a group of young *paniolos,* or cowboys, who had moved away from the main body of the party and were laughing and singing together some distance away.

Larry and Cyrilla sat on as well, silent in the night, just listening to the music and enjoying the performances. It was obvious that they were comfortable in each other's company; Larry kept his arm around his wife; Cyrilla rested her curly salt-and-pepper hair on Larry's shoulder.

Finally, near midnight, tired parents gathered up sleeping youngsters and began bundling families into cars. Those who were staying overnight began to drift inside. Larry and Cyrilla moved off to wish people good night, but still Derek sat on in the quiet night. Beyond the roof overhang, he could see the stars twinkling overhead, so bright he was sure he could just reach up and touch them. He felt peaceful and tired, and more than content.

Chapter Seven

Bright sunlight flooded his face when Derek opened his eyes the next morning. A soft knock had awakened him from dreams of Lani—and there she stood, staring around the door at him, laughter in her eyes.

"Want to have a ride before breakfast?"

As she moved into the room, he saw that she was dressed in jeans and a loose T-shirt, her long hair pulled back with a wide ruffly twist. She looked beautiful.

As he continued to just lie there staring at her face, she narrowed her eyes at him. "You do ride?"

A slow smile slid across his chiseled lips.

So it really was Lani standing beside his bed, not just a continuation of a pleasant dream. "Why, honey, you're looking at a Texas cowboy, here-ah," he drawled. " 'Course I ride."

With a quick grin, she turned and fled the room, calling out behind her that she'd be waiting in the kitchen. "And don't forget to bring your swim trunks."

Left with that intriguing order, Derek hurried out of bed to get ready.

It was still early enough to be cool, but the sun on their backs was already warm as they set off. Towels, a thermos of hot coffee, and a napkin full of bread rolls were bundled in the saddlebags of Lani's horse.

Lani was in a wonderful, happy mood. Since neither of them had ridden much recently, and Derek was getting to know a strange horse, they set a slow pace.

Lani showed Derek some of her favorite spots—special childhood places, like the grove of guava trees where she'd pick fruits to nibble and the little hollow at the base of the mango tree where she'd settle in with a good book.

As they stopped for a while beneath the old mango tree to have some coffee and rolls,

Derek shared stories about his own private childhood spots, telling her about the tree house he and his father built one summer and about the little creek where the neighborhood boys went skinny-dipping.

"Speaking of skinny-dipping," Derek said, a twinkle lighting his eye, "I brought my swimming trunks."

"Good."

Lani smiled, but didn't elaborate. Instead, she gathered up the remains of their breakfast and returned to the horses.

Derek could hardly believe this was the same woman he'd encountered at the airport less than two weeks ago. That woman had been stiff and formal. But today, he actually thought she was flirting with him. It was a feeling he enjoyed.

He wondered if the relaxed atmosphere of the ranch was responsible—or just the relaxed clothes. There was that old saying about clothes making the man. Before she'd appeared yesterday in jeans and a T-shirt, he'd only seen her dressed for work. Perhaps she shed the professional guise with the clothes. Her work-clothes were very businesslike, like her attitude while wearing them. In her jeans and casual tops, she seemed freer, happier, and definitely more carefree.

As his mind roamed back over their past meetings, he was startled to realize how few there had been: that first day, of course, at the airport; at her office the next day when he'd gone in with the injured Justin, and again after work for dinner; and then in the grocery store on Friday.

Goodness, they had been together only four times.

He looked over at some shrubs brightened by clumps of red berries, only half listening as Lani told him they were called Christmas berries and they used them in their holiday decorating. He was too busy considering what implications there might be in the fact that he'd seen her only four times and yet could hardly get her out of his mind.

When he brought his full attention back to the present, they were riding beneath tall eucalyptus trees, planted many years ago as a windbreak along the edge of a wide pasture. As they steered the horses beneath the branches of bluish leaves, the faintly antiseptic scent given off by the trees tickled their nostrils.

"Do you have a sudden urge to suck on a cough drop?" Derek asked, turning his face up and sniffing again.

Lani laughed, but repeated his action. "I love the smell of the eucalyptus. It always makes me think of home."

She looked around her, her eyes taking in the sloping green pastures, the distant cattle, and the towering mountain above them. Her eyes turned even darker as they roamed the familiar sights, and a faint smile tilted her lips.

Then, seeming to shake off whatever thoughts had overcome her, she turned back to Derek, smiling brightly at him.

"Now, the moment you've been waiting for," she announced. "I wish I could produce a drum roll."

She had to laugh when Derek obliged by rolling off a string of *ta-ta-ta tums*.

"See those trees up ahead?" she asked, pointing to a thick grove of trees. "There's a beautiful little pond there with a waterfall. It's a perfect swimming hole." Her voice dropped as she confided, "It's one of my favorite places."

Within minutes the horses were tied up and they were walking along the well-worn path through the guava and *waiawi* trees. The chattering of the birds, chased from their foraging among the ripening *waiawis,* was gradually superseded by the sound of running water. Derek, carrying their towels and the thermos with the last of the coffee, followed Lani, listening as the sound of the water grew louder.

The sight of the pretty little pond burst upon the senses with the suddenness of a beautiful sunrise.

One moment they were plodding along the path through the heavy brush, the next they stood before a clear blue pool, nestled at the base of a small waterfall. Short but wide, the water tumbled over swiftly enough to produce a white mist at its base. Huge gray rocks rose up around the pool, peeking out from the thick green vegetation. Up beyond the guava trees, the greenery thickened. Towering *ulu* and spike-leafed *hala* trees created what appeared to be an impenetrable forest upstream.

"Wow."

Derek's quiet exclamation thrilled Lani.

"The stream goes underground from here and comes out in the pastures about a half mile away. That's why it's just this little pond."

"It's beautiful. It looks like a movie set."

Lani smiled her pleasure at his reaction. With a wide grin she led him to the edge of the pond. There was a large, clear rock there where clothes could be spread, and clear entry into the water.

"We can leave our things here," she said, indicating the large, flat stone.

Suddenly, Lani felt shy. It was hard letting someone see you in a swimsuit for the first time—especially someone like Derek. He was a handsome man, a celebrity, actually. He was used to partying with the most beautiful women in the world. And here she was, a country girl, with short legs and a less than impressive figure. Insecurities she'd thought left behind her resurfaced with a vengeance.

Clenching her jaw in resolve, she unfastened her jeans and pulled them off, the oversized T-shirt still covering her to her thighs.

She was glad to see that Derek, following her lead, was also removing his clothes. While that occupied him, she pulled off her T-shirt— quickly, before she lost her courage entirely.

When she turned back to Derek, she was struck momentarily by the sight of his strong, athletic body. Distracted, she didn't see the way his eyes flared in appreciation when he saw her in her simple one-piece suit.

For just a moment, both Lani and Derek stood in silence, each appreciating the appearance of the other. Then Lani seemed to recollect herself, grinned at her companion, and jumped feetfirst into the pool. Within seconds she surfaced. With a shake of her head that sent her long hair flying, she tread water and grinned at Derek.

''Come on in. The water's fine.''

Derek grinned back, moving to the edge of the pond where she'd entered.

''How deep is it?''

''Deep enough to dive. Jump in feetfirst though. I'll race you to the other side.''

Before he had a chance to respond, she'd flipped over and started out.

''No fair,'' he called. But he was already leaping off the rock, his competitive instinct aroused.

The pond was small, and Lani was a strong swimmer. His greater height and strength were helping him catch up, but he had to work hard to beat her by an arm's length.

They came up near the waterfall, warmed by the exercise, engulfed by the water mist. It was shallower here, and they could stand with their heads out of the water.

"You cheated," Derek began. But he was laughing as he said it. After all, he'd won anyway.

"I was just evening the odds," she explained with a grin. "You're taller and stronger. I deserved a handicap."

They stood together in the cool water, warm now and soothing as it moved over their skin. The laughter they shared brought them closer, and the magic of the setting began to exert its power.

Lani's smile sobered as she looked at Derek's evenly tanned shoulders. He had dropped down into the water so that their eyes were at a height. She was looking right into his gray eyes, eyes that were rapidly losing their laughter and taking on the blue color of the water and sky.

Lani shifted in the water. Derek stood close beside her and she fancied she could feel his warmth, radiating outward into the cool water. It was traveling the short distance across to her, flowing over her body, warm and wonderful.

Derek thought Lani looked terrific. Her long hair was wet, springing into wavy strands that framed her oval face. She was smiling, a dreamy look on her face as she stared into his eyes. Her salmon lips were slightly parted, an invitation he found impossible to resist.

With the water warm and sensual swirling around them, he leaned forward and placed a kiss on her lips.

Surprised, captivated by the soft kiss, Lani's feet slipped on the slick rocks that made up the bottom of the pond. She fell forward. Derek's arms came up to catch her, holding her captive in his warm embrace.

The sound of the waterfall hummed in her ears—until she realized it was her own heartbeat she heard, so loud and strong it filled her senses. Then she pulled back and away from Derek in a panic, swimming beneath the waterfall.

The roar of the water meant she didn't have to talk, and the pounding of the water brought her back to her senses. She'd been indulging in some sort of dream, and now she was back in reality.

Derek followed her, his strokes long and smooth. He was relaxed, enjoying himself. But he knew the moment was gone.

He watched Lani play beneath the waterfall,

floating on his back just beyond her. She belonged here in this beautiful island setting.

What a change she was from the tall, leggy blonds he'd always considered his "type." The models he often dated wore tiny bikinis when they went to the beach or to a pool. But they just sat beside the water and asked him to help with their lotion. He suddenly realized that they never wet more than their feet. None of them would ever have put her face into the water much less raced him across a mountain-fed pond.

So he shouldn't be surprised at the sudden shyness Lani was showing. The conservative one-piece suit she wore should have been a tip-off.

But if she was surprised by her unexpected reaction to his kiss, he was stunned. The sweet temptation created by her lovely lips had drawn him. But the shot of heat he felt from that honeyed kiss was as amazing as the first glimpse of the beautiful little pool had been.

Derek continued to drift casually, floating on his back, his eyes on the towering greenery and the blue sky dotted with clouds above. But he was fully aware of Lani, of where she was in the pool, of what she was doing.

He felt like a teenager on a first date—that was how she affected him. And from the way she was steadfastly staying a full length away from him, she was as confused as he was.

Lani also swam at a leisurely pace, back and forth across the picturesque pool while her mind moved along at far greater speed.

The casual kiss Derek had dropped on her lips was anything but casual to her. She could still feel his lips against hers—damp from his recent immersion, cool. Yet the impact was all dry heat.

Her arm reached out, pulling at the water in long, smooth, even strokes.

How could such a small, apparently mean-ingless action of his create such havoc in her? True, he was incredibly good-looking. But she'd never dated someone just because of the way he looked. Other things were much more important.

And she wasn't sure she wanted to be in-volved with someone who was so eagerly pur-sued by the tabloids. In fact, she knew she didn't!

Another trip across the pool brought her troubled mind no closer to a resolution. But she knew she couldn't stay here forever, swimming back and forth, trying to work it out. The puffy white clouds that had been drifting across the sky all morning were beginning to gather into masses of gray-white. Lani recognized the signs. It would begin to rain soon.

Several quick, strong strokes brought her back to the spot where she'd entered the water. In seconds she was out and wrapped in a towel. Shivering slightly, she reached for the thermos of coffee.

By the time Derek stood dripping beside her, there were two cups of still-warm coffee poured out. Lani offered one to Derek with a smile.

''We have to get going before the rain starts. This will help warm us up.''

Pink tinged her cheeks as she realized that other things as well could warm her—like his kiss. But to her relief, Derek accepted the cup with no comment, instead turning his eyes skyward to check her weather forecast. And Lani filed away a special memory, to be ignored but never to be forgotten: a sweet, warm kiss shared in a cool mountain pool.

Chapter Eight

Lani escorted her friends down the narrow sidewalks of Lahaina and into the entrance of The Lone Wolf.

"I can't believe you got us in here." Valerie, always exuberant, was particularly so today. It was a combination of seeing her old friend again and newlywed bliss. "We heard at the hotel that it was almost impossible to get dinner reservations unless you called days in advance."

"I didn't want to let down my best girlfriend." Lani gave her a fond smile before stepping up to the hostess.

Valerie's husband winked at Lani. Doug was

a tall, good-looking man with shocking red hair and a pale complexion already reddened after one day in the tropical sun. "She probably knows the owner and gave him a call."

To the surprise of both Doug and Valerie, Lani turned bright red. She was relieved that the hostess took that moment to speak, asking them to follow her upstairs.

Her friends waited until they were seated at a prime bay-front table and had given their drink orders. Then Valerie pounced on Lani.

"Now, give. What was that strangled look you got when Doug suggested you knew the owner? Isn't this place owned by that football guy? The hunk who had to retire because he wrecked his knees?"

"Yes." Lani thought her voice sounded choked and too throaty. "Derek Wolfe."

The waitress was already back with tall glasses of iced tea. Lani welcomed the reprieve as well as the drink. She took a quick sip of her tea, swallowed, then returned the glass to her lips for a good long gulp. She just knew Valerie would read more into her relationship with Derek than was actually there.

What relationship, she reminded herself. They were mere acquaintances.

Lani realized that Valerie and Doug were waiting for her to continue. ''I met him at the airport when I was picking up Uncle Charles.''

''So you *do* know him!''

Lani's eyes met Valerie's, but she ignored her friend's squealed comment. ''You remember Uncle Charles.''

Valerie nodded. She and Lani had been college roommates for all four of their undergraduate years, and she had spent one glorious summer with Lani at the ranch.

''Uncle Charles finally took some time off and went to visit his daughter on the mainland last month. He decided that with me here to cover for him at the office, it was time to visit his grandkids in their own home.'' Lani smiled in remembrance of all the photos she'd admired since his return.

Then she shrugged and returned to the topic that interested her friend. ''He and Derek Wolfe's mother sat together on the plane from Los Angeles. They've become great friends,'' she added.

Valerie squeezed up her mouth in concentration. ''It's hard to picture Uncle Charles dating.'' She turned to her husband to explain. ''He's like someone from another generation,'' she said. "He's very formal and he has such exquisite manners. I hope you get to meet him before we go."

"He's not a real uncle," Lani told Doug. "He and my dad grew up together, and have remained close. Mark and I have always called him uncle."

Refusing to be sidetracked by mention of Lani's older brother—the brother she'd had such a crush on all those years ago—Valerie grabbed Lani's hand. She held on to it as she returned to the subject that most interested her.

"So tell us," she said, her eyes sparkling with merriment. "What's the great Derek Wolfe like? Is he as good-looking as they say? Is he wonderful? You deserve a great guy after that jerk Ron. I never really liked him. And he scared you off men—you haven't dated at all since you broke it off with him, have you? And that was years ago."

Lani shrugged, taking another sip of her tea. She didn't want to talk about Ron, didn't even want to *think* about him. A fellow student in medical school, Ron was one of the worst memories she had of that time. He'd embarked on a whirlwind courtship near the end of their first year. She'd been blissfully in love. It

wasn't until after the engagement, with wedding plans already underway, that she'd un-
derstood about Ron. He was interested in
himself, and only himself. He'd wanted a wife,
an intelligent, hard-working wife, who would
go out and work and pay for the rest of his
education. When she broke it off, he'd worked
his charm on another student, married her, and
talked her into quitting school to take a job in
a research lab.

Lani shook off the melancholy memory and
took another sip of the refreshing tea. Valerie
was still talking.

"Well, you deserve a really nice guy. Now
that you're done with your residency, you'll
have time for dating."

Lani laughed. "I don't know about that."

But Valerie barely heard her. "So tell us
about the football hunk."

Lani took another sip of tea, grateful for the
alert waitress who kept her glass full. She
didn't understand why her throat was so dry
this evening. But she did wish the conversation
would take a turn. She wouldn't mind discuss-
ing the best beaches on Maui or the flower gar-
dens at Kula. Her heart plumented to her knees

when Doug looked around the room and made his casual comment.

"There's the fooball hero now. Looks like he's working the tables."

Valerie and Lani followed the direction of his gaze. While Valerie babbled in excitement at actually seeing the big hero, Lani felt herself grow warm. The light ocean breeze so recently blowing through the room seemed to disappear, its cooling properties lost.

Lani hadn't seen Derek since he'd dropped her back at Uncle Charles's house after their stay at the ranch. On the drive back they'd talked and laughed, and even sung along with some oldies on the radio. Their easy acceptance of each other's company had made the weekend magical.

Lani thought of it as the most wonderful weekend she'd ever had. For the past week she'd been pulling out memories of it. They helped her through the long early morning drives and the disruption of late-night calls. Especially enjoyable were the images of them riding out on horseback together, laughing together.

But she tried hard not to remember their swim in the idyllic pool. Thoughts of that moment led only to that casual kiss—which had been anything but.

So was she ready to face him again? Would Derek in the flesh support her beautiful memories?

Derek was immediately aware of Lani's presence in the dining room. Even if he hadn't known she was coming, he would have been aware of her. No workclothes tonight. She wore a deep red muumuu that made her skin glow and added to her exotic beauty. And her long hair was loose, the dark waves tumbling over her shoulders.

Derek couldn't understand why he was so sensitive to Lani's presence. Although she was lovely, she wasn't the prettiest woman in the room. There were a pair of middle-aged businessmen at the table before him with two world-class beauties sitting beside them. All four were overdressed for the casualness of a Lahaina bar-and-grill.

Derek frowned as he turned away from the table after greeting them. The two women were the type he usually dated, the kind of women who looked like they'd just stepped off the pages of a fashion layout. Tall, beautiful, elegant, worldly—all the words men like himself, his friends, and the two insurance men at the table used to describe their ideal dates.

Derek found himself distracted as he visited with a family from San Jose. The twelve-year-old boy wanted his autograph and he complied. Not to be outdone, his eight-year-old sister had to have one too. But although he signed his name and made small talk, Derek's mind remained on the young doctor near the back of the room.

When Derek broke away from the family, he went straight to Lani's table. Why fool himself? He might not understand her appeal, but it was there and impossible to ignore. He wanted to say hello, to sit at the fourth chair at their table and visit for a while. In fact, he wanted to be invited to join their party.

"Lani."

Derek came up beside the table and placed one hand on her shoulder. Giving in to an irresistible impulse, he leaned over and placed a light kiss on her cheek. He had to smile at the flushed confusion on her face as she returned his greeting. Without the kiss, of course.

"Hello, Derek. I'd like you to meet some friends of mine—Valerie and Doug Sullivan.

They're visiting from Santa Barbara. They're on a delayed honeymoon.''

''Well, congratulations.'' Derek shook hands, then lowered himself into the empty chair at the table. ''You don't mind if I join you for a minute, do you?''

Lani wanted to say yes, she did mind. He made her nervous in an elemental way she didn't want to explore. But she could see that Valerie was thrilled to be seated at the same table as the ''football hunk.'' Even Doug seemed thrilled to meet Derek, and he didn't seem worried about his wife's adoration.

''Please do.'' Lani cleared her throat. Her voice sounded oddly husky. ''I see the restaurant survived the weekend without you.''

Derek smiled. ''Yes. Gordon did a great job. I have a good group of people working for me.''

Derek went on to explain to Valerie and Doug about training his assistant, about their trip to the ranch, and the success of the experiment.

Lani tried to ignore the speaking look from Valerie when the trip to the ranch was mentioned, but, to her relief, the subject changed after that and conversation became easy.

The men discussed football for a while, with Valerie an interested listener. Lani tried to look interested too, but distractions were everywhere. She could catch the masculine scent of Derek's aftershave, something she remembered from their long car ride together. When he shifted his long legs, his knee brushed hers— even that quick touch turned her leg to flame.

Her throat was so dry she took a huge mouthful of water and choked on the icy drink. Sputtering and coughing, she felt even hotter as Derek alternately slapped and rubbed her back.

"Are you all right?"

Her three table companions watched her in concern.

"What happened?"

The questions came so fast and tumbled over each other so that Lani hardly knew who had asked what. All she was aware of was the proximity of Derek Wolfe—and the eyes of the entire room watching as she coughed and choked, practically in his arms. Last time was bad enough. She wondered how many of the employees remembered her previous visit. Now this.

If not for her friends, Lani would have retreated from the restaurant in sheer embarrassment. As it was, she swallowed hard, cleared her throat, and tried to look enthusiastic about the appetizers that arrived about the same time she stopped coughing.

Derek was about to suggest he join them for dinner when he saw the hostess in the doorway gesturing for him.

"Excuse me, but something seems to have come up." He rose, nodding to Valerie and Doug. "Nice to have met you. Enjoy your meal."

Then he turned to Lani. She almost choked again on a bite from a potato skin when she looked into his eyes. Surely he wasn't going to kiss her again.

Derek's eyes sparkled as he clapped a hand over Lani's shoulder and gave it a squeeze. "I'll see you around," he said, then hurried toward the hostess, who was now looking slightly frantic.

In a moment the entire dining room knew why she appeared that way. A statuesque blond with an unbelievable figure entered the room like a whirlwind. She posed in the doorway just long enough for everyone present to notice, then practically launched herself at Derek.

Derek put his arms around her in a reflexive action that caught her to him in a close embrace.

"Derek."

Her voice reminded Lani of Marilyn Monroe. Breathless and fluty, it floated over the heads of the fascinated diners.

"Derek," she repeated as Derek released her. "That person told me you were working." She gave a pretty pout as she gestured back toward the hostess, then wrapped her arms around Derek's. The pout became a sultry smile. "I told her you'd have time for me."

Derek bowed his head close to her ear, his voice low, difficult for anyone to overhear. Everyone was trying, though. Not a fork clinked, not a cup rattled. The restaurant was absolutely quiet.

Whatever he said, the pout returned to her red lips. But she backed away from him—not *too* far away, Lani noted—and walked with him to a small table in the back corner.

Slowly the restaurant came back to life. A low buzz of conversation quickly grew louder, and the usual clicks and clangs of china and flatware began once more.

"Wow," Doug began, his eyes still on the beautiful blond.

"Oww." Doug's eyes moved quickly over to Valerie, who'd just kicked him under the table. "What was that for?"

Valerie took a bite of her potato skin and chewed carefully before answering. "For looking with too much pleasure at that"—she paused while she searched for an appropriate word—"floozy."

"I didn't," he protested.

Lani smiled at the two of them. "You two are supposed to be on your honeymoon, Doug, even if you have been married for six months. She doesn't even want you to look."

She tried to relax as the conversation finally turned to sight-seeing. But she was all too aware of Derek's continued presence in the room. Sitting at an intimate table with the most gorgeous woman she'd ever seen. Their heads were so close together a hand couldn't pass between them.

Just as their dinners arrived, Derek and his companion left. Lani tried hard not to notice. But how could anyone not notice that the attractive woman was clinging to him once again, as though she needed support to walk in those towering heels.

Lani rebuked herself for being petty. What upset her most was the fact that Derek and the ''floozy'' made such a beautiful couple.

Chapter Nine

Lani didn't care if she never saw Derek Wolfe again. If she'd ever had doubts, she now felt sure that his womanizing reputation was earned.

She sat in the living room with Uncle Charles this evening, her legs folded under her in a corner of the couch, an open pediatrics journal in her lap. She and Charles had sat down together after dinner to watch a movie on television, but Lani quickly lost interest in the thin story line and picked up the journal.

But even though her eyes remained focused on its pages, her mind kept drifting back a week ago to her dinner with Valerie and her husband. And to Derek and Ms. Tiffany Tarrington.

She'd discovered the name of the voluptuous blond she'd seen at the restaurant just that afternoon. As she waited in line at the grocery checkout, she'd scanned the headlines of the tabloids on display beside her. Usually, the extraordinary claims on the front page brought a smile to her lips.

But there was no smile today when a large colored photo caught her attention. For there was Derek, coming out of The Lone Wolf, the beautiful blond clinging to his arm. It must have been taken the night she'd seen them; the blond, an actress named Tiffany Tarrington, wore the same clinging tomato red dress she remembered. The caption intimated that the former football star and the actress were heavily involved.

Lani pulled her mind away from dismal images of Derek and the beautiful actress when she realized that Uncle Charles was talking to her. Apparently he'd given up on the movie too.

"I'm sorry. What was that?"

Uncle Charles smiled at her. In recent years Uncle Charles had become a very serious man, concentrating on his work until he'd become a classic workaholic. But he was smiling more and more these days, turning back into the happier man he had been before his wife's long struggle with terminal cancer.

"You were a million miles away, Lani." The smile changed to a frown. "Not a difficult case, is it?"

Lani used the term "difficult case" when faced with a patient with a life-threatening problem. Drowning, brain tumors, and leukemia sometimes claimed her little patients, but, thankfully, not too often.

"No, it's not that." Lani closed the magazine in her lap and put it aside. "I am distracted tonight though. What were you saying . . . ?"

A brilliant smile lit his round face, and numerous wrinkles appeared in the corners of his eyes. "Barbara and I are going for a ride out to the Iao Needle this weekend. With some friends."

"That should be nice." Lani, still distracted by thoughts of Derek, found it difficult to get excited about a sight-seeing trip. But the way he grinned when he mentioned Barbara—now that was something to think about.

"Yes. I'm really looking forward to it. I haven't been on a motorcycle in years."

Lani sat up straight, her legs flying out from under her to settle with a flat-sounding thump on the carpet. On its journey to the floor, her right foot hit the journal she'd placed on the coffee table and tumbled it to the floor as well. Lani didn't even notice.

"A motorcycle?!"

Charles didn't seem the least bit perturbed at the thought of riding a motorcycle at his age. For a man as serious as he was—or had been, for the past eight-odd years—he was acting positively bubbly.

"Yes. When I was your age, all I had for transportation was a motorcycle." His head moved back and forth at the fond remembrance. "Then I got married and had to get a car.

"But some of my friends from the old days still ride. They belong to a motorcycle club and they've been urging me to get a bike again and join them. They ride all over the island—husbands and wives. Sometimes they even go on trips on the other islands. They visit all the scenic spots. It sounds very nice. Barbara and I are looking forward to it."

Lani swallowed. Pictures of motorcycle accident victims she'd seen during her emergency room rotation in medical school clouded her vision and caused her breath to catch in her throat. Only Uncle Charles would call a motorcycle trip ''very nice.''

''Does Barbara have a motorcycle?'' She tried to picture short, slightly chubby Barbara on a motorcycle.

''No. Actually, I'll be borrowing one for this trip. If I enjoy it, then I'll get one of my own.''

Lani's mental picture changed. However, the thought of Barbara riding tandem was even more ludicrous than the idea of her on a bike of her own. But then Lani couldn't even picture Uncle Charles on a motorcycle.

Charles, off on a nostalgic mental trip, surprised Lani with a long sigh. ''Boy, I remember that Harley I had. What a bike that was.''

''A Harley?'' Lani almost wished she could go back to visions of Derek and the actress. The word *Harley* brought forth grade-B movie images of big black motorcycles and rough, rowdy, leather-jacketed riders. Emergency room memories resurfaced.

''Oh, yes. I had a beautiful olive green Harley. Got it used, but it was a good bike. Very reliable. I might like to get one again. I'm sure I haven't forgotten how to handle it.''

''I suppose it's like bicycles,'' Lani said. At a quizzical look from Charles she elaborated. ''You know, everyone always says you never really forget how to ride a bicycle?''

''Ah, yes.''

Charles smiled, a wide pleasant smile that made Lani feel guilty about her desire to see the outing canceled.

Lani tried to settle comfortably back into the couch again. But no matter how glad she was to see Uncle Charles so happy, the thought of the aging man on the back of a motorcycle upset her.

Did Derek know what his mother was planning? And did he approve? He seemed to care deeply for his mother. So how could he condone this? Lani knew she was doing exactly that herself, but how could a thirty-year-old woman tell a sixty-two-year-old man what he could and couldn't do? It was different with Derek and his mother. An older woman would expect her grown son to watch out for her. Wouldn't she?

Lani excused herself, leaving Charles to the television. He'd given up on the movie and found a nature program on the public television station.

In her bedroom, with the door closed, Lani tried to call Derek, but was unable to reach him. Unbidden, an image of the beautiful actress appeared in her mind—the lovely Tiffany Tarrington and Derek Wolfe entwined together in a semblance of a dance.

Lani shook the picture from her mind.

She spent a restless night, interrupted twice by worried mothers checking out symptoms they felt sure were dangerous. So when Lani climbed out of bed on Saturday morning, she was feeling tired and grumpy.

The games were well under way—Special Olympians from all over the island were competing in track and field events. Lani stood near the finish line as the winner broke the tape. The wide smile on the child's face proclaimed her happiness at her victory in the race. Lani hugged her before releasing her and passing out hugs to all the other participants. The kids had done a great deal to cheer her up after her dreary night.

As Lani moved back, waiting for the next event, she was surprised to hear her name. Actually, it wasn't the fact that someone had shouted her name that surprised her. But she recognized the voice that called it out. What was Derek doing here? Her smile turned to a frown.

She saw him as soon as she turned, his size making him immediately noticeable. As a warm feeling flooded her, Lani chided herself for her inevitable reaction to the handsome man. Many sports figures lent their support to the Special Olympics. He had every right to be here. As much as she did, maybe more.

Derek strolled over to stand beside her, his long-legged stride quickly covering the distance between them.

"Boy, you are one hard lady to track down."

Derek looked down at Lani's face. She wore sunglasses, so he couldn't see her eyes, and her hair was pulled back with a clip in her usual no-nonsense hairstyle. But the wind had pulled out wisps all around her face, giving her an impish look that was captivating. He badly wanted to touch the curling tendrils. He pushed his hands into the pockets of his slacks instead.

"I've been calling you all week. You're always busy or with a patient or at the hospital.

Do you work all the time?'' His voice sounded sincere. He really wanted to know.

After years of single-minded concentration on her studies and her future goal, Lani suddenly felt defensive about her workaholic lifestyle—for the first time ever. ''I take time off now and then.''

Derek knew she was prevaricating and wasn't about to let her get away with it. ''I mean other than your visits to your parents' ranch.''

Lani shifted from one foot to the other. ''This is fun.''

Derek looked around. There were children everywhere, in all sizes, all shapes. He could see the signs of organization behind the apparent chaos though. But he shrugged. ''Maybe.''

''Are you one of the volunteers too?''

Derek looked uncomfortable. ''Not really. Mama took her car in for some minor adjustment so I dropped her off at your place. Charles said you might be out here.'' He took another look around.

Lani was flattered that he'd come specifically to see her, but his mention of Uncle Charles reminded her of the trip her beloved mentor was on. "Speaking of Uncle Charles," Lani began.

But a child in a wheelchair rolled up to them at that moment, bestowing a big smile on them both before focusing his attention on Derek. "You're the Lone Wolfe."

Derek smiled at the young boy and took his hand for a shake. "That's right. Are you a football fan?"

As he talked, he squatted down so that he was at the child's level. Lani was impressed at the easy way he communicated with such a special child. Some adults never were able to feel comfortable talking to children. But Derek was being friendly, as he might be with an adult who approached him, but at the child's level. And that crouching position had to be hard on his bad knees.

When the boy rolled away, a personalized autograph clutched in his hand, Derek rose to his feet. A quick flash of pain passing through his eyes and firmly controlled was the only indication that he wasn't as perfect as he looked. Lani suddenly wondered if he always wore long slacks to hide the thick scars around his knees that she'd briefly seen the day they had gone swimming together.

"That was very nice of you," Lani commented.

Derek shrugged off the compliment. "It was nothing. He was a sweet kid."

His eyes followed the child as he wheeled himself away.

Suddenly, Derek began to notice, really notice, the children scattered over the field. Some, like the child leaving, were in wheelchairs. Some wore leg braces. Many others showed limitations of various kinds. Yet they were competing like any other athletes, proud of their abilities and their accomplishments.

Derek Wolfe, with his no longer perfect body, suddenly felt small. Feeling an unexpected desire to help, he asked Lani what he could do.

The morning passed swiftly. Derek stayed with Lani, helping out wherever they were needed. The children—and perhaps even more so, their parents—were happy to meet the famous former football star.

And Lani saw a whole new side of Derek Wolfe. This was a man she was proud to know. The question of Charles and Barbara, off sight-seeing on a borrowed motorcycle, was completely forgotten.

Later, Derek followed Lani to a nearby fast-food outlet where they ordered large soft drinks and sat down to talk. Lani removed her sunglasses as they settled down at a table, a large order of fries between them to share.

Derek frowned at her. Again.

"You look tired."

"And you're beginning to sound repetitive." Lani removed the paper from her plastic straw and punched it through the plastic cover on her drink. Her thoughts returned to her earlier worry.

"I tried to call you last night. You're not so easy to reach yourself."

Derek shrugged but had the grace to look embarrassed after accusing her of the same thing earlier. "I, uh, had to entertain an old friend."

"Miss Tarrington?" Lani tried to catch back the words, but it was too late.

If Derek thought the comment catty, he wasn't obvious about it. He raised one eyebrow, though, which gave him a very debonair look.

"So you recognized her that night in the restaurant. Tiffany would be happy to know that.''

He didn't seem like someone in love. His voice conveyed something much more like distaste.

''Well, not really.'' Lani found she couldn't lie about it. ''Actually, I saw a photo while I was standing in line at the supermarket. . . .''

Derek grimaced. ''Tiffany's only interested in her career. She was on Maui for a photo shoot. She's angling for a swimsuit calendar. She came by that night hoping the photographers would follow. And it seems she got exactly what she wanted.''

Glad to know he and the actress weren't ''heavily involved,'' Lani buried all jealous thoughts, completely forgetting about the ''old friend'' previously mentioned and the fact that he hadn't exactly answered her question. She had more important things on her mind.

''Have you heard about this trip Uncle Charles and your mother are on?''

Derek didn't bother with his straw. He removed the top from his cup and took a good long sip. ''Mmm, that feels good. It's hot today. And yes, Mama told me all about it.''

Lani's eyebrows rose at his calm acceptance

of his mother on the back of a motorcycle. Derek didn't seem to notice her reaction.

"I'm glad Charles is taking her around a little. I've been so busy with the restaurant since we moved here that I haven't had time to do the tourist things with her."

"So you don't object to her riding tandem on a motorcycle?" Lani couldn't help but express her surprise at his urbane attitude. After all, she wasn't happy thinking of Uncle Charles on a motorcycle. And this was his *mother*.

"Motorcycle!" Derek's voice was loud enough to make several heads turn their way. With a conscious effort, he brought it back down to conversational level. "What are you talking about?"

Lani had to smile, which caused Derek to frown fiercely at her. She was beginning to get used to that frown. It made him look kind of cute.

"Well, I wondered how you could be so blasé about it. They're going sightseeing all right. With a motorcycle group Uncle Charles knows. It seems he had a bike years ago—a Harley. And he thought he'd like to get another, now that he's looking at retirement. So he's borrowing one from a friend for this trip.

If they have a good time he's going to buy himself another Harley-Davidson.''

Derek's mouth formed a silent whistle. ''Uncle Charles on a Harley.''

''Boggles the mind, doesn't it?''

''What does he wear when he rides?'' The thought of the elegant old gentleman in denims or black leather was beyond his imagination. But the thought of Mama . . .

''And Mama's planning to ride tandem?'' He slammed his fist down onto the table, causing Lani to jump almost a foot into the air, spilling several fries out of their container, and sending another round of curious looks their way. ''What am I going to do with that woman? First a sports car and now this. She's going to kill herself.''

The frustration in his voice touched Lani. He really cared about his mother, but he didn't know what to do to help her.

''Please, calm down.'' Lani glanced quickly around the room. She hated being the center of attention.

''That's exactly the way I feel,'' Lani admitted. ''But they're adults. I guess we'll just have to give them our support and pray for their safety.''

Derek stared at Lani. "You're serious, aren't you?"

Lani shrugged. "I'm terrified every time I think of them on that motorcycle. But Uncle Charles has friends in the group who are his age, and they and their wives have been doing this for years. And the traffic on Maui isn't anything like it is in California." Lani pulled out all the rationalizations she'd thought of to comfort herself since last night. "Besides, what else can we do?"

Derek shifted into gear and stared out at the roadway through narrowed eyes. Lani might feel she had to step back and leave Charles and Barbara to themselves. But he had no such compulsions. After all, Charles was not a blood relative of Lani's, just a good friend of the family and an honorary uncle.

But this was his mom they were talking about. He couldn't let her continue on this way. Tennis was one thing, though he'd even worried about that. After all, she was fifty-six years old and had never done anything more athletic than plant tulips. He'd insisted she see the doctor for a checkup before she started her lessons, just as a precaution.

Then she'd wanted a fast sports car. It was not physically difficult to handle, but certainly life-threatening in other ways.

And now a motorcycle. At the rate she was going, she'd kill herself before the end of the year. Even though the doctor had said she was in excellent health.

Back in his office, Derek dialed his sister on the mainland. "Tracey, I'm going to send Mama off to you for an extended visit."

"Well, hello, Derek. How are you? I'm fine, thank you, but the baby has a cold."

"Okay, okay." Derek pulled a pencil from the silver cup on his desk and wove it through the fingers of his free hand. He heaved a long sigh. "I'm glad you're fine. How's the rest of the family?"

The usual family small talk relaxed him a little and a grin tugged at his lips. "Little Mikey keeping you up with his sniffles?"

"Yeah, we did have a rough night. Everyone else is healthy at the moment." Derek could hear childish chatter at the other end of the line, including one high, thin whine that grew louder and louder. "Just a minute."

Voices filtered through; he caught a word here and there including "Uncle Derek" and

"Grandma." Then Tracey's voice was back, still cheerful. "So what's this about Mama?"

Derek launched into a detailed explanation of what had been going on, and his concerns that Mama was endangering herself with all this new activity.

"She seems to think she's a teenager again, Tracey." The pencil he'd been playing with suddenly snapped into two pieces. He threw them down in frustration. "What am I supposed to do? Lani says we should give them our support and pray for their safety. But I think Mama should go over for an extended visit with you. Stay through Thanksgiving. Maybe Christmas."

Tracey's voice was still cheerful, but more interested. "Lani?"

"She's sort of a niece of this guy Mama's been seeing."

"Mama's been seeing this Charles you mentioned?" Tracey's curiosity fairly bounced across the phone lines. "And how can she be sort of a niece?"

So Derek launched into an explanation of Lani and Charles and their unique relationship.

"He sounds like a marvelous old guy,"

Tracey announced when Derek finished. "Why is there a problem?"

"Your mother, and mine, is bouncing around the island riding tandem on a motor-cycle with a sixty-year-old man who hasn't rid-den one in twenty years or more—and you ask where's the problem?"

In his agitation he took another pencil from the cup to run through his restless fingers. It lasted all of twenty seconds before snapping in two like its predecessor. Derek threw it across the room.

"I think you're taking it all too personally, Derek. Mama's a grown woman and it isn't up to us to decide what she can do or not do." Derek heard her murmuring to one of the kids before she spoke to him again. "So tell me about you and Lani."

"There is no me and Lani."

"Uh-huh." Tracey's voice had that smug I-know-something-that-you-don't-know tone that had always irritated him when they were kids. "Are you dating?"

"No." There. He'd said that in a nice firm tone of voice that would squash any romantic notions she was entertaining. "I just took her out to dinner once to apologize for knocking her down at the airport. And I drove her out to her parents' place one weekend.''

Over in South Bend, Tracey was laughing. Even the sound of a crash wasn't enough to stop her. But she did end the conversation. ''I've got to go. Something just happened in the kitchen. Talk to you soon.''

Derek sat there staring at the telephone, the dial tone loud in the quiet room. His life was really going downhill fast. Women kept hanging up on him, something pretty well unheard of until recently. He put the receiver back into its cradle and glared at the pale instrument for a while. Then he said a silent prayer for Mama and left the office. She hadn't said anything about him picking her up. But he might just do it anyway.

Chapter Ten

Lani was surprised to hear the doorbell when she stepped out of the shower. She'd gone from feeling grumpy and upset early this morning to a pleasant relaxation this evening.

After her enjoyable morning with the children and with Derek, she'd come home, changed into her oldest jeans and spent the rest of the afternoon gardening. She liked the feel of the damp soil between her fingers and the basic scent of the overturned earth. The unstructured nature of the time spent outdoors among the flower beds had done a lot to reduce the stress of a busy week.

Now, fresh from the shower and feeling like

a new person, she wrapped a white terry robe around her still-damp body and hurried to the front door. Uncle Charles must have forgotten his key.

But Lani stepped back in surprise when she opened the door. It wasn't the medium-size figure of Charles Wong standing on the porch outside. The waning light might be behind him, but she'd recognize that shadow anywhere.

"Derek. What are you doing here?"

Derek could only stare. Lani's hair fell in damp curls around her face and over the collar of her robe. It was a short robe, and he found it hard to take his eyes off the long expanse of golden legs that showed beneath it. Lani might not be tall, but she was beautifully proportioned. Thoughts of Mama on a motorcycle flew out of his mind as he found himself distracted, and floundering for words.

"I, uh, guess Mama's not back yet."

Lani found herself returning the stare of the handsome man before her. The admiring look in his eyes was obvious and flattering. It made her feel very feminine and very beautiful.

For uncounted seconds, they stood together in the doorway, one in, one out. Words seemed unnecessary as each enjoyed the presence of the other. The fragrant perfume of tropical flowers drifted in from the garden to mix with the spicy scent of Derek's aftershave and the clean floral smell of Lani's soap.

The sound of an approaching car broke the spell.

Shaking herself from the sensual trance induced by the emerging dusk and Derek's charismatic presence, Lani stepped forward, putting her hand on Derek's arm to keep him from storming out to meet Barbara. Instead, she invited him inside.

"Come in and wait for them. I didn't know you were picking Barbara up," she added. "When I heard the bell I thought Uncle Charles had forgotten his key."

Derek had the grace to look embarrassed. "Well, she didn't ask me to. I just thought it might be a good idea."

Lani had to smile. There might be some fireworks when Barbara came in and saw her son.

But the meeting went smoothly. Derek had managed to calm himself and seemed as reluctant as Lani to bring up the question of the motorcycle ride. And Lani was feeling self-conscious in her short robe. So after a few quick, meaningless social comments, she escaped into her room to change.

It wasn't until she'd pulled on a short muumuu and brushed her hair that she realized Barbara probably thought Derek was there to visit her. The quick smile Barbara had passed between them when she entered the room should have been a giveaway. Lani blushed now at what the older woman must have thought about her state of dress—or undress.

By the time Lani reentered the living room, Charles had invited Derek to join them for dinner and gone outside to fire up the barbecue. Lani found Derek and Barbara sitting tight-lipped on either end of the sofa.

"So . . ." Lani began. She looked from mother to son and decided Derek must have made some remark about the motorcycle ride. She flashed a bright smile. "Can I get you something to drink?"

Two quick no's put her back where she'd begun. She sat in the chair beside the sofa. "So, Barbara, how was your excursion?"

Lani flinched inwardly at the false brightness in her voice, but Barbara didn't seem to notice. She turned to Lani with a sincere smile and told her how much she'd enjoyed the day trip.

With no comment on their means of transportation, she spoke of the lovely park and the lively company of ''Charlie's'' friends.

Charles entered the room from the kitchen just in time to hear her glowing report on his friends. His smile made Lani's heart glad.

''They're a good group, aren't they? I'm so glad you enjoyed meeting them.'' Then, with a gesture at the blue-and-white striped apron covering his clothes he added, ''I've lit the coals, and the teriyaki's been soaking since last night. It shouldn't be too long.''

''And I have everything ready for the salad,'' Lani added.

''Charlie,'' Barbara said. ''I was just telling Lani how much I liked Roy and his wife, Pam. Such nice people. We should get together with them again sometime. They play golf together. . . .''

As Charles moved closer to Barbara to continue the conversation, Lani stood up and motioned to Derek. ''Come on and help me with the salad, won't you?''

She waited until they were in the kitchen together before confronting him. ''What on earth did you say to your mother? You two looked like you wanted to kill each other when I came into the room.''

Derek stuck his hands into his pockets and paced away from her. But it was a small kitchen and he was back facing her in less than a minute.

''I just asked her why she didn't tell me it was a motorcycle trip.''

One side of Lani's mouth pulled down as she gave him a skeptical look.

Derek felt defensive and he didn't like it.

''In that nice tone of voice?'' Lani asked.

Derek gave in. It must be his destiny to be taken to task by petite women—first his mother, now Lani.

''I might have used a stronger tone,'' he admitted.

''Oh, Derek.'' Lani shook her head at him. ''And she probably said she didn't tell you because she knew you'd react just like that.''

Derek didn't like the way she could read his mind either. ''I thought we had to make a salad.''

''Okay, okay.'' Lani opened the refrigerator door and began to hand him things. ''I rinsed out lettuce and greens earlier, and peeled and cut the carrots and celery. All we have to do is slice the avocados and arrange it all on a plate.''

The atmosphere in the kitchen lightened, and by the time Charles and Barbara came in for the meat, Derek and Lani were laughing together at the counter beside the sink.

The evening progressed better than it had started. Charles talked a lot about the trip and how much he'd enjoyed it.

''There's just nothing like a motorcycle. The wind in your face, the freedom. I'm sure it must be like flying your own plane,'' he said.

At first Barbara cast fretful looks at Derek, as if wondering if he would explode at their host and create a scene. But the somber, earnest air that surrounded Charles imbued the talk with a calm composure that soothed the safety concerns of the younger people.

After the meal, they returned inside to escape the worsening mosquitoes. While Barbara helped Lani in the kitchen she spoke in a low, confiding voice.

''Thank you for talking to Derek.''

She brushed away Lani's protest. ''I know you must have said something to him. He was having one of his macho fits about the trip before you went off into the kitchen with him.

After that, he was fine.'' Barbara smiled at Lani. ''You're a good influence on him.''

Lani gave Barbara an impulsive hug. ''And you're a good influence on Uncle Charles. He looks so much happier and healthier since you two have been seeing each other.''

To her delight, Barbara blushed.

''He had been working much too hard, you know,'' Lani continued. ''It was affecting his blood pressure. But these last few weeks— why, he's been practically a new man.''

Barbara was spared a reply when the men came in from cleaning up out back, noisily claiming the kitchen sink to wash up.

''I was just telling Derek about Thanksgiving at the ranch,'' Charles told Lani as he turned away from the sink and wiped his hands. ''I've always had one of the doctors here in town cover for me that weekend so I can spend Thanksgiving with Lani's parents at their ranch,'' he explained to Barbara. ''It's a beautiful place, just ask Derek.''

As Derek agreed with Charles about the Kalimas' ranch, they seated themselves at the kitchen table while Lani brought a chocolate cream pie out of the refrigerator. She poured coffee into cups and distributed them around the table before sitting down herself.

"Since this is my first year back, I haven't had Thanksgiving at the ranch in years." Lani's voice was thick with longing. "I can't tell you how much I'm looking forward to it."

"What are you folks doing for Thanksgiving?" Charles asked.

Barbara looked to Derek, who shrugged. "I hadn't really thought about it. We'll go to a restaurant at one of the hotels for dinner. I *have* decided to close The Lone Wolf for Thanksgiving—so my employees can spend the day with their families."

Lani, still feeling emotional over her wonderful memories of Thanksgivings past, couldn't stand the impersonal nature of his plans. Especially when he was being so considerate of his employees.

"You can't do that," she blurted out without thinking. As her cheeks turned pink at the way her remark sounded, she tried to smooth it over. "I mean, you should have a nice dinner with friends, or family on Thanksgiving. Look, why don't you come with us. Mom won't mind, and there's plenty of room for you to stay."

With Charles happily echoing the invitation, Barbara was quick to accept. But Derek looked into Lani's eyes, as though trying to determine the reason behind the invitation.

Lani stared right back. "You have your assistant to take over for the rest of the weekend, don't you?"

Derek nodded. "Yes. He's more than competent. It's just . . ."

But he seemed to reconsider whatever he'd meant to say. Instead he smiled at Lani and accepted her invitation.

When they left shortly afterward, Barbara was gushing with excitement at the idea of spending the four-day weekend at the ranch. Lani, though, suspected her attitude had more to do with the thought of spending the time with Uncle Charles than with the opportunity to see a working Hawaiian ranch.

Lani wished she could feel that same excitement about spending the time with Derek. Their last weekend, only a day and a half long, had been wonderful—so wonderful she sometimes doubted her memories.

So what would happen this time, amid the hectic preparations of the holiday, with all the numerous family and friends about?

There was no way to know. And Lani hated the unexpected.

Thanksgiving morning dawned clear, with a bright sun promising a beautiful day. Even Haleakala, often shrouded in clouds, appeared in all its green and brown glory.

Lani was up, staring toward the open window as the first streaks of pink began to emerge on the horizon. Propping up the pillows, she lay in the disheveled warmth of sheets and blankets and enjoyed the pleasure of being home, of lying in bed to enjoy a sunrise, and the unmitigated luxury of four whole, unscheduled days ahead of her.

As early light brightened the room, Lani let her eyes roam over familiar objects, settling at last on the quilt covering her bed. Bright red on a white background beginning to yellow with age, the intricate stitching depicted leaves and flowers radiating outward from the *piko* or center of the quilt.

Lightly her fingers ran over the fine stitching. The pattern was called ''The Beauty of Maui'' and the quilt had been made many years ago by her grandmother. An avid quilter, Lani's grandmother had left several quilts to her daughter, Lani's mother. In accordance with the Hawaiian tradition, Cyrilla brought them out for special occasions. Lani had felt tears in her eyes last night when she saw the quilts spread out on her own and the guest room beds.

Cyrilla, ever vigilant to her daughter's moods, had spotted the tears Lani immediately attempted to blink away. Leaning close, she'd spoken in a low voice, close to her daughter's ear. "Only the best for my daughter and her friends."

It wasn't just the fact that the quilts were saved for "best" that had made Lani so emotional. This particular quilt was special to her. As a child her father had often referred to her as his "Maui Beauty." It had made this quilt special too when she'd learned its name, back when she was four years old. Cyrilla still told the story of the imperious little girl who'd announced that it must be her quilt as she was her Daddy's Maui Beauty. When the quilt came to Cyrilla upon her mother's death, she had promised it to Lani upon her marriage.

For the first time in years, Lani wished a marriage was in her near future. Her fingers stilled over one of the quilted roses as a shadowy picture of Derek floated into her mind. The strange daydream made her blush as pink as the morning sky. With a quick flick of her wrist, quilt, blanket, and sheet were thrown back, and Lani stepped out of bed.

Lani scolded herself as she pulled clothes out of dresser drawers. What on earth was she thinking? She'd decided long ago that marriage would have to wait. Much as she would love to have a husband and children of her own, she felt a responsibility to establish herself as a practicing physician and repay her loans first.

But scolding herself couldn't distract her from the origins of such thoughts. Hadn't she just spent a restless night dreaming of a handsome former football player?

She shivered in the early morning chill. Pulling on jeans and an old cotton shirt of her brother's, she brushed her hair and quickly made the bed.

Once again her hand slowed as she smoothed it over the cotton fabric. The beautiful quilt symbolized family life to Lani. Although she was still young when her grandmother died, Lani clearly remembered the sweet old woman. She always had full cookie jars for the grandchildren, and she took time to explain her ever-present stitching to the curious children. Memories of the woman and her lifestyle were sewn into the quilts she left behind.

With a final tug at the quilt and a sad smile, Lani left the room. A quick breakfast and a long ride were just what she needed to get her mind back on track. Career first, personal life second.

Some little incongruity in her thinking pricked at Lani, but she decided to ignore it. Years of careful planning couldn't be tossed aside for a sudden brief attraction—no matter how appealing the object of the attraction.

Derek awoke early, the rich aroma of coffee snaking through the house to tickle his nostrils. He'd spent a restless night that had little to do with the too short bed in the Kalimas' guest room and everything to do with the petite doctor down the hall.

A quick shower did little to dispel the dream pictures of Lani that had haunted his night, though he turned the spigot until the stream of water turned icy cold.

Sweet, pretty Lani Kalima was really getting to him.

*   *   *

Derek entered the kitchen as Lani finished pouring herself a cup of coffee. She wished him a good morning, trying to ignore his rugged good looks and the attractiveness of the damp hair that curled over his ears, a shade darker than its usual wheat gold.

"Good morning, Derek," Cyrilla called out from the other side of the long room. A large turkey sat on the counter before her and the scent of onions and other less identifiable herbs and spices filled the room. "What would you like for breakfast?"

"I'll get something, Mom," Lani offered. "You're busy."

She turned to Derek, offering him the cup of coffee in her hand. She could get another for herself. "What would you like?"

"Some cereal would be fine, with fruit if you have any," Derek said. "And more of this," he added, nodding toward the cup from which he'd already taken a sip. "Good coffee."

"Thank you," Cyrilla answered. "There are some nice papayas there on the counter, Lani. Use those."

They had a leisurely breakfast, though they

both offered numerous times to help with the meal preparations. Finally, when they'd finished their coffee, Cyrilla pushed them toward the door.

"Why don't you two go for a ride? I'm used to having the kitchen to myself. Having other people around . . ." She waved her arm, indicating the large room as though it were filled with people. "They just get in my way and make it harder. You can help clean up," she added as she saw Lani ready to protest.

Lani had to laugh. "Okay, okay. We'll stay out of your way this morning and help clean up after the meal." She leaned over to place a kiss on her mother's flushed cheek. "But you be sure and call for me if you decide you need an extra pair of hands."

By the time they returned from their ride, washed up, and reentered the kitchen, the room was almost unrecognizable.

When she was a girl, Lani remembered going with her parents to visit friends in their new house. She'd been terribly impressed at the small dining room they had, just like ones she'd seen on television programs. For years, Lani had thought that her ideal home would have just such a dining room. Now, infinitely wiser, Lani gazed about the warm kitchen and knew this was the ideal.

Filled with furniture, people, and the most mouth-watering aromas, the old kitchen could have been a set for the old *Waltons* show on television. Men, women, and children were talking and laughing, passing platters and bowls to the table, inching their way around the perimeter of the room.

Extra leaves had been added to the old oak table so that it filled the large room from counter to counter. This enlarged table was completely surrounded with several different styles of chairs, the place settings as close as possible and as diverse as the chairs. Every spare inch of the rest of the table was covered with dishes, platters, and serving bowls, all brimming over with delectable foodstuffs.

"Wow." Behind her Derek had expressed everyone's opinion of the opulent spread. "Cyrilla, did you do all this yourself?"

"No, no. Everyone contributed something." Her smile widened at the appreciation on his face and she gestured everyone forward. "Come on, come on, take your places. Let's eat before it all gets cold."

With noisy good humor, everyone took a place at the large table, Larry intoned the blessing, and the bowls and platters began to move from hand to hand.

Later, stuffed to the point of lethargy, chairs were pushed back and the older people moved outside to the large porch. A guitar and a couple of ukuleles appeared and within moments the soothing sound of Hawaiian music drifted through the open windows and into the kitchen. Lani and Derek and all the other young people shortened the table, returned the borrowed chairs, washed the dishes, and put away the leftovers.

Derek hadn't done dishes since he was a kid, but he found himself enjoying the camaraderie of working with Lani and her relatives. They laughed and joked and teased. Much of the teasing had to do with him, but he found he didn't mind. It was all so good-natured, he found himself teasing back. With everyone encouraging him, he stole quick kisses, flustering Lani, which was almost as much fun.

By the time they moved outside to join the others, the sky was an incredible coral, and the earth shimmered with that unique color that appears just before the sun sets. The grass seemed greener, the roses that grew along the front of the house a richer shade of pink.

Derek sat on the steps, pulling Lani down beside him. Her cheeks were as rosy as the flowers beside them, and he plucked a blossom to present to her.

''For you, Lani. A lovely flower for my lovely Maui rose.''

Lani wanted to laugh at the corny comment, but it just brought more color to her cheeks. He grinned. ''Now I know what it means when some poet says a woman has roses in her cheeks.''

He reached up with the flower, intending to put it in her hair. Instead, as he twisted it between his fingers getting ready to tuck it behind her ear, he yelped.

''Ouch.''

Lani laughed, even as she took the blossom from his hand. ''Funny thing about roses. They have thorns.''

Derek joined her laughter. ''Is that a warning?''

Lani didn't reply, just settling in beside him, resting her head lightly against his shoulder. She held the delicate rose to her nose, breathing deeply of its sweet fragrance. The silky petals grazed her cheek, and she let out a soft sigh of contentment.

Relaxing against Derek, Lani's gaze moved through the gathering dusk. Quietly she poked Derek in the ribs with her elbow, nodding toward the swing in the shadowy corner. Barbara and Charles sat together, heads close, speaking in low tones.

Derek frowned at them, eliciting a chuckle from Lani. "So I'm not the only one you frown at that way."

Derek turned to her, eyebrows raised. "Do I frown at you?"

"All the time. I'm starting to get used to it." *I'm starting to like it*, she added to herself. It meant he cared about her and about what she did.

"I'll try to remember to smile instead," he told her, tightening his arm around her and pulling her closer to his side.

Sitting behind them in the Adirondack chairs, Cyrilla and Larry looked at each other and smiled.

Chapter Eleven

Derek pulled into the driveway of Charles's house and parked the car. Charles and Barbara, dressed in their tennis whites, were sitting together on the small porch talking and laughing.

"Derek." Barbara got to her feet, looking at him in surprise. "What are you doing here?"

Derek shrugged, wondering himself why he'd driven out to Charles's place.

Thanksgiving weekend had been one of the most enjoyable times of his life. These last few days, as he coped with the day-to-day problems of his restaurant, he'd found himself missing the easy camaraderie he'd enjoyed with the Kalimas. He missed the long discussions with

Mama and Charles over tall glasses of iced Kona coffee. But most of all he missed the company of dark-haired, sloe-eyed Lani. Bright, funny, serious—she was so many different women; she fascinated him as no other woman had been able to do.

He gave his mother a sheepish grin. "I thought I'd come out, see if I could catch Lani, maybe take her out for some dinner."

Barbara's grin was wide. "Great idea. Charlie has his American Legion meeting tonight. It's a dinner meeting," she added.

As she finished speaking, all three turned at the sound of another car entering the drive. Because Charles lived at the end of a residential dead-end street, drive-by traffic was rare, and noticeable. As they all watched, Lani climbed from the newly arrived car.

The smile of greeting that sprang to Derek's lips at Lani's appearance died. He noted her slumped figure as she turned to retrieve something from inside the car. Her weary smile, offered to them all as she climbed the few steps to the porch, looked forced. What he'd planned as a smile of welcome turned into a frown.

"Are you all right?"

"Of course." Lani followed her answer with

another limp smile but Derek found it no more convincing than the first. Apparently his mother agreed, for she stepped closer to Lani and enclosed her in a hug.

"Hard day, honey?"

Derek watched as Lani closed her eyes for ten seconds, seemed to recollect herself, then returned the hug. "Pretty bad." She swallowed hard before speaking. "Had a little boy rushed in during lunch. Only seven months old. Drowned in a backyard kiddie pool."

Her lips pinched together tightly as she saw once again the beautiful child, his head covered with long dark curls, probably never cut. "They started CPR, got him breathing again. He might make it," she added, her voice dropping to a near-whisper. "But he'll never be the same."

She moved away from the little group to deposit her purse and bag on a chair. When she turned back to them her arms were wrapped around herself, her knuckles showing white as she gripped her upper arms. She offered a shaky smile. "You're not supposed to get emotionally involved, but in cases like this . . ."

"It's okay." Charles had risen when she arrived and now he put his arm around her shoulders. He, more than anyone, knew what she was going through.

Charles seemed to lend some of his solid strength to the younger doctor, for she settled into a more relaxed posture, her hands now gripped loosely before her.

Derek came to a quick decision. ''You shouldn't be home alone tonight. Why don't you go in, have a nice relaxing bath. Bubbles and oil and all that stuff. I'll come back in an hour and pick you up. Tomorrow's your day off, right?''

At her nod, he continued. ''We'll get some dinner, maybe see a movie—something cheerful and distracting. What do you say?''

Derek flashed his best, most charismatic smile. The one that always melted the ladies. Except it seemed to have no effect on this one. Her eyes met his, refusal written clearly in their brown depths. But before she could respond, Charles and Barbara were heard from.

''What a good idea!'' Barbara exclaimed at the same moment that Charles said, ''That's just what you need, my dear.''

Three pairs of eyes turned to her expectantly. Lani sighed and nodded. She was too tired to argue with all three of them. ''I'll just go get into the bath. That part *does* sound good.''

An hour later, Derek once again stood on the porch of the old house, his hand raised to knock on the door. It opened before his knuckles had a chance to touch the wood.

Lani stood before him, dressed in a deep blue muumuu, her hair lying free over her shoulders, but held back over one ear with a spray of white dendrobiums.

''Lani.'' Derek found himself stopping to catch his breath. Belatedly he proffered the single long-stem pink rose he'd brought for her. ''You look beautiful.''

Lani had to smile as she put the rosebud to her nose and sniffed its sweet fragrance. He was sweet himself. And the appreciation she could see in his eyes made her feel particularly beautiful.

''Thank you.''

With effort, Derek forced himself into a lighter mood. ''Ever since Thanksgiving, whenever I see a pink rose I think of you.'' Color bloomed in her cheeks and his lips curved into a smile. ''There they are, those pretty pink roses,'' he teased.

Lani laughed as she invited him in. "I see you had all the thorns removed from this one."

She didn't wait for a reply, moving into the kitchen to put the flower in water. She returned quickly, set the rose in its bud vase on a table, and collected her purse and sweater.

Derek took her elbow as they walked down the steps to the car. Lani was thanking him again: ". . . for forcing me into a decision about this evening. I lay in the tub until the water turned cold—and I felt so much better afterward." She smiled up at him before sliding into the car.

As Derek got behind the driver's seat she admitted, "I feel human again. And looking forward to the evening. I can't remember the last time I saw a movie."

Derek started the engine. "I hope you won't be disappointed, then, because instead of a movie I thought we'd go to the Maui Arts and Cultural Center in Kahului. They're doing *Joseph and the Amazing Technicolor Dreamcoat.* It's a Broadway musical. . . ."

Lani laughed. "I know. I'm not *that* out of touch. But how ever did you get tickets? I heard it was all sold out."

"I can't tell you all my secrets. But I do have contacts."

Lani laughed at the tone of voice he affected for this last pronouncement. "I'll just bet you do."

Derek raised his eyebrows at her comment, but declined to pursue it. "However, it means we'll have to eat afterward. There isn't time to stop now." He was already turning out onto the highway that would take them to Kahului.

"No problem." Lani's eyes clouded over momentarily. "I'm not hungry."

Several hours later, Lani could happily take back her words. As they settled into Derek's table at The Lone Wolf she declared herself to be starved.

"Oh, Derek." Her eyes sparkled with laughter and her lips tipped upward even as she spoke. "That was really the best show. It was so funny."

Derek had to return her smiles. "It was okay."

Lani gave him a stern look. "Now don't tell me you're going all sophisticated on me. I loved it, even if it wasn't *Les Misérables.*"

Derek smiled. "Sophisticated? Me? Why

I'm just a midwestern Hoosier country boy, ma'am.''

Lani's laughter seemed to fill the room. She was so beautiful, male eyes kept turning their way, but the musical sound of her laughter had even the women glancing over to smile at her.

Lani was grateful to Derek for helping her through a difficult day. The more she got to know him, the more she liked him. She was discovering that Derek Wolfe was not the cardboard figure of a playboy portrayed by the tabloids. He cared about family and friends, could joke about himself. He liked to ride and was considerate of the animals. In other words, he was an average person—a fairly nice average person.

Their waitress approached with a big smile for the boss and his guest. Lani agreed on the fish special, then tuned out as Derek continued to speak to the young woman about their order.

Thanksgiving weekend had been wonderful, not only because she'd spent it at the ranch with her family, but because Derek had been there to create more memories with her. They'd enjoyed many long rides, several picnics, and had joined Charles and Barbara on treks to local scenic spots.

Lani had to smile as she recalled how Charles had lamented the fact that he no longer owned a motorcycle, a lack he planned to remedy soon. Lani bit her lip whenever Charles spoke of the joys of riding and was glad to see that Derek did the same. He did, however, talk to Charles about his views on the wearing of helmets.

When she brought her mind back to the present, Derek was watching her intently.

"Are you all right?"

Lani blinked, then offered a smile. "Yes. Just woolgathering."

Derek looked relieved. "Good." He gave a shaky laugh. "When you didn't answer me, I got a little worried."

He didn't say it but Lani knew he thought she was dwelling once more on thoughts of the tragic little drowning victim. But she'd put that behind her.

"Actually, I was thinking of what a nice weekend we had."

Derek was quick to agree. "I can't remember a better Thanksgiving myself." He grinned at her. "I usually had to work."

They talked a little about his life as a football player, then moved on to the show they'd just seen. The conversation took them through soup and salad.

Lani admitted to little experience at viewing live theater. ''I've been so busy these past years, I hardly even got to see any movies. And the few I watch now are on television.'' She didn't mention that theater tickets were beyond her limited medical student budget.

Their entrées arrived and they remained silent as they tasted the perfectly grilled fish fillets. After short comments on the excellent food, Derek moved the conversation to her career. ''How did you decide to become a doctor? Was it Charles's influence?''

''Not really. Not at first.'' Lani took another bite of asparagus before continuing. ''My cousin was very sick when we were young.''

Lani put down her fork and sighed. ''It's a long story.''

''In that case, wait until you finish eating.''

With a deftness born of years of social experience, Derek kept up a steady stream of small talk while they finished their meal. Then, over coffee, he returned to the topic.

''Okay. Now that it won't interfere with your meal, tell me the long story of how you decided to become a doctor.''

Lani smiled at him. He really was the nicest man. It just went to show that you shouldn't rely on first impressions.

"When I was young, Uncle Bill lived in the house where Mark lives now. He's Dad's brother," she explained. Lani added some milk to her coffee and continued to stir the mixture as she spoke.

"Uncle Bill and Auntie Eileen had one son. They'd tried for a long time to have a baby and Auntie Eileen just doted on him." She put the spoon aside and held her hands around the cup as though she needed the extra warmth.

"They named him William Kalima, and called him Will so he wouldn't be confused with his father." With her two hands still around the cup, she brought it up to her mouth and took a sip.

"Then he got sick. Very sick. He had to go to the Shriner's Children's Hospital in Honolulu for treatment and having him there just about killed Auntie Eileen. She would go to visit, staying with relatives. And the visits got longer and longer. Finally she didn't come back. Eventually Uncle Bill decided to move to Honolulu permanently, so the family would be together.

"It was the visit to see my cousin in the hospital that did it for me. I was only ten or eleven and I was terribly impressed. All those wonderful nurses and doctors, caring for those sick children, making them better." She met Derek's eyes across the table. "That was the key. Willie was so sick, but they had made him so much better. I decided right then that that was what I was going to do when I grew up."

Derek nodded. It was no more than he had expected. What a caring person she was. She'd probably saved baby birds too, out at the ranch.

Now that she'd shared one of the most personal details of her life, Lani felt shy. She ran her fingers along the fabric of her muumuu, pushing the cloth into tiny pleats. She kept her eyes on her lap, waiting for Derek to say something.

Derek didn't say anything. But his next action did surprise her. He reached over and placed his finger under her chin, exerting a gentle pressure until her head came up and she met his gaze.

Warmth radiated through her at his gentle touch. His changeable eyes turned a darker shade of blue as he continued to gaze upon her lovely face. Slowly his head lowered.

Lani stared into Derek's face. She felt hypnotized by the intensity of his eyes. And they grew larger and larger. . . .

Her eyes widened in alarm. Surely he didn't mean to kiss her. Not here in the restaurant!

Already more than aware of him because of the light touch beneath her chin, she felt a sudden rush of heat that stained her cheeks pink as she pulled away from him.

Derek straightened back in his chair. He'd been momentarily hypnotized by his tender feelings for a beautiful woman. Now he'd embarrassed her.

With a quick movement, he pushed back his chair and stood. ''Time to get you home.''

Since he didn't look into Lani's face, Derek missed the disappointment she quickly hid. It *was* late. But she felt regret at ending such a delightful evening.

Chapter Twelve

Once again Lani was rushing through the grocery store on her way home from work. There was no particular reason for the mad rush; she just hated to waste her precious free time in the supermarket.

Waiting at the checkout, impatient for the line to move forward, she let her eyes scan the racks of tabloids. Was Derek on the cover of any of them this week?

The woman in front of Lani moved her cart forward, having finished emptying her groceries onto the counter. But Lani remained where she was, her eyes wide, her lips parted in horror.

There before her in large black letters was the headline ''The Jock and the Doc.'' And below it, in living color, a photo of Derek— and herself!

The picture was slightly grainy in the way of photos shot over a great distance with a telephoto lens, but there was no doubt about the identity of the couple pictured.

Her hand trembling, Lani reached out for a paper, just as the man behind her reminded her to move forward. Folding the offensive paper over, she added it to her groceries and hastily deposited them on the counter.

Moments later, in the privacy of her car, Lani opened the paper and stared at the front page. She and Derek were standing close to-gether—*very* close together—beside a horse. They were staring into each other's eyes in a way that implied intimacy. It looked like they were going to kiss. Or perhaps had just kissed.

Indignation flooded through Lani, staining her cheeks with spots of bright color. There must have been a photographer hiding some-where on the ranch over the Thanksgiving hol-iday. They'd gone on many rides together, alone and in groups. But they had not kissed.

The photo provoked an image of a relationship that did not exist.

Her cheeks grew even hotter as she remembered their first ride together. Thank goodness they'd gone on their recent excursions in the early morning. It was cool then and they hadn't been tempted to swim as they had that first weekend. The thought of a lurking photographer hiding in the ample coverage provided near the swimming hole . . .

Lani couldn't even complete the troubling thought.

Once again she folded the paper over so that the photo didn't show. Then she stuffed it into one of the grocery sacks. Her hands were unsteady as she inserted the key and started the engine.

Backing out of the parking slot, she felt as though passersby were staring at her. She had to fight the impulse to look between the parked cars for lurking paparazzi. It was her imagination, of course. But it was bothersome.

Was this how Derek felt? All the time? How did he cope with it and yet manage to be so normal?

It wasn't until she pulled into the driveway of her home that the worst aspect of the photo hit her. How would this affect her practice? What would the reaction be—and would it cost her patients?

And her parents!

Lani exited the car, slamming the door hard behind her. It helped to release some of the anger and frustration she felt. But not near enough.

Derek swore, quickly apologizing to his mother. She'd just entered his study, dropping a tabloid-size newspaper before him on his desk.

Another muttered expletive sounded, this time too soft for Barbara to distinguish.

''I can't believe this. Just when things were going so well too.''

Derek stood, walking from the desk to the window and back again. He was finally getting somewhere with Lani. Over the long weekend he'd felt she was warming up to him, really getting to *like* him.

And now this.

He stopped at the desk, picking up the paper and examining the photo. ''Lani will hate this.''

Barbara just stood beside the desk, in the

same spot where she'd been since she dropped the paper before him. Her eyes were clouded with concern. "What will you do?"

Derek threw the paper down and wished he could get his hands on the paparazzo who had gone sneaking around on private property to catch them during their ride.

"I don't know, Mama. I'll go over and see her." He looked once again at the large photo. "He must have been hiding on the ranch somewhere over the weekend. I wonder how he knew I was there?"

But he knew it was a rhetorical question. He hadn't made any secret of where he was headed for the holiday. But he'd never been pursued like this either.

He stuck his hands into the pockets of his chinos and walked around the desk until he stood beside Mama.

"The worst of it is, all our rides were so innocent. That picture makes it look like we were having some kind of intimate rendezvous. And it was just a lucky shot by a good photographer."

"I know, dear. But Lani doesn't have our experience with these people. Maybe you'll have to explain."

Derek sighed. "I know I'll have to explain. I just hope she'll listen."

Barbara gave her son a hug. "All you can do is try. I'll be over later. Charlie and I had planned to rent a movie."

Derek returned his mother's hug. He knew she wanted to help. But this was something he'd have to tackle alone.

The doorbell rang just as Lani hung up the phone after talking to her parents. They had already heard about the photo, courtesy of friends who'd seen it and immediately telephoned. They offered their loving support, and a place to stay if she felt the need for a few days off.

Feeling emotionally drained, she headed to the front of the house to answer the door.

A gentle rain was falling, the gray sky matching her dismal mood. Derek's large frame filled the doorway, his lips tipped downward in his usual frown of concern. His eyes were clearly gray today, another reflection of gloom.

"Are you all right?" A quick look into her eyes seemed to confirm the fact that she'd seen the current paper. His voice gentled. "I'm really sorry, Lani."

His arm went around her shoulder, but Lani noticed he seemed reluctant to embrace her. Was he embarrassed to be associated with a country bumpkin like herself?

She forced a laugh. "I guess this is a real switch from your usual image."

Derek kept his arm around her as he led her from the porch to the white plastic love seat set under the mango tree on the side lawn. The misty rain was almost unnoticeable, and beneath the thick-foliaged tree, the love seat was dry. "What are you talking about?"

Lani shrugged, effectively shaking herself from his grip. "You know. I'm quite a comedown from the usual glamour girls you're featured with. Actresses, models . . ."

Derek shook his head, trying to reorient himself. He'd expected anger at the paper and embarrassment at the photo and its publication. He seemed to be getting jealousy—not altogether bad, but certainly unexpected.

Derek took Lani's shoulders in his hands, turning her to face him.

"Lani, you're the most beautiful woman I've ever known. You're beautiful both inside and out, not shallow and superficial like some of those glamour girls you're referring to.''

Lani stared into Derek's eyes. She could see flecks of blue in the gray now as he stared earnestly across the short distance between them. Neither of them noticed the rain, which continued to fall, misty and light. It gave the landscape a dreamy quality, blurring the bright colors of the tropical growth and cooling the heat of angers and jealousies.

''You think I'm beautiful?''

Lani's voice was so low she wasn't sure Derek would even hear it. But it was the most she could manage at the moment.

''The most beautiful woman in the world. I love you, Lani Kalima.''

Lani could only stare. He loved her. Maybe that photograph wasn't such a lie after all. Perhaps the photographer had caught something between them that they hadn't been aware existed. Or that they'd been reluctant to admit existed.

''I love you too, Derek.''

There in the shadows of the mango tree, Derek gathered Lani into his arms and shared a gentle kiss.

''Will you marry me?''

His warm words, whispered in her ear, shattered Lani's newfound happiness. Marriage. Family. Her dream. But too soon. Too soon.

With an incoherent cry, she raced out of his arms and into the house. She barely avoided being hit by Uncle Charles, whose car was just pulling into the drive.

Charles parked, exiting his car with alacrity. He looked toward Derek, walking slowly across the lawn. The rain was turning into a heavier drizzle and dark spots were beginning to appear on his shirt.

"What's wrong?"

Derek just shook his head as he followed the older man into the house. He didn't reply until they were seated in the comfortable living room, a lamp lit to overcome the growing gloom.

"I don't get it. I told Lani I loved her and asked her to marry me."

Derek still looked stunned by the progression of events. Charles broke into a smile.

"She said she loved me. Then she suddenly pulled away and ran into the house."

Charles's smile disappeared. He knew Lani very well, and he had a good idea of the reason behind her action. But it wasn't his place to explain.

"I'm sorry. I like you. I think the two of you make a fine couple. But I don't want to interfere."

Derek's eyebrows flew up in surprise. "You mean, you know what's going on?"

Charles expression remained serious. "I have an idea, yes. But you will have to talk to Lani. Work it out between you. It is not a big problem, I think, even though she believes it is."

With this enigmatic pronouncement, Charles rose and left the room.

Derek sat quietly for a moment as the dark closed in outdoors, listening to the increasingly hard raindrops pound on the roof. Finally, he came to a decision.

Rising from the sofa, Derek headed down the hallway. He knew which room belonged to Lani from the night he'd driven her home from the restaurant, and he went there now. He gave a brief knock and walked in.

Lani lay on top of her bed, her back to him, her face buried in a large pillow. Her body shook though he couldn't hear any sobs.

Derek walked over, sitting on the bed beside

her and lifting her in his arms. He held her close.

"We need to talk."

The bedroom was growing dark, the white bedspread almost glowing in the increasingly dim light. Sitting on the comfortable bed, Lani's incredibly warm body in his arms, her head nestled into his shoulder, was too much for Derek. He knew they had to get out of there.

He brought her to her feet, took a handful of tissues from the box beside the bed, and put them in her hands. Then he led her out of the room.

By the time they entered the kitchen, Lani looked like herself again, except for the reddened eyes. Derek turned on all of the lights, then rummaged around in the cupboards until he found a kettle.

"What are you doing?"

Lani, still bewildered by the way her life was getting away from her, stared at him as if he'd gone crazy.

"I'm going to make some tea." He put the water-filled kettle on the stove and turned to face her. "You do have tea, don't you?"

Lani nodded, going to the cupboard for the

can of tea bags. Then she got out the teapot, cups and saucers, spoons and napkins. It felt good to do something.

Derek stopped her after she filled the sugar bowl and was preparing to fill the creamer.

''All that isn't necessary. I take it plain,'' he added, then snatched the kettle off the fire as it started to whistle. He filled the teapot with boiling water, but let Lani handle the rest of the preparations. She apparently needed to be doing something with her hands.

Finally, she'd done all she could do, and was left with just her own cup to hold.

Lani arranged the cup on the saucer just so, then smiled brightly at Derek. ''So.''

Derek looked at her, his expression somber. ''So,'' he repeated, echoing her tone as well. ''You didn't answer my question earlier. Should we be planning a wedding?''

Lani looked down into her teacup. She'd used tea bags, but there were still loose flakes of tea at the bottom of her cup. If only they would tell her something. She sighed.

''I don't think so.''

Derek pushed aside his cup and took her hand. ''I love you, Lani. I've never said that to anyone before.'' He gave a short laugh, hoping to lighten the mood. "Unless you count Mama."

Lani smiled at his quip, but she still refused to look at him.

Derek tried again, squeezing her hand between his two. "You said you love me," he reminded her. "Why won't you marry me?"

Lani extricated her hand from his, dropping it into her lap to grip its mate. "I do love you. It's just that my life is complicated right now, Derek." She finally raised her eyes to his. "I just don't feel like I can put myself and all my problems into someone else's life right now."

"What problems?" Derek refused to give up so easily. "I'm sure we can work things out if you'll just talk to me about it."

At the front of the house, they heard the door open, then voices. Barbara must have arrived for her television date with Charles.

Lani was shaking her head.

"You can't tell me?"

"It's just so hard."

"Try."

Lani put her hands back on the table, twisting the cup in its saucer. "It's just that I have all these debts, from school and all."

She stopped him as he started to interrupt.

''I know. You're going to say you'll take care of it. But that just doesn't seem right. I need to get on my feet on my own.''

Derek just looked at her for a moment. Foolish as this seemed to him, it was just like Lani. She was really very old-fashioned about a lot of things.

''And are you?'' he asked. At her quizzical look, he elaborated. ''Getting on your feet on your own?''

''Yes. But slowly.'' She frowned at the teacup. ''If this publicity doesn't ruin my practice.''

''Then I don't see the problem,'' Derek said. ''We'll announce our engagement—very publicly, tomorrow. Or tonight even. Then there won't be any suspicion of hanky-panky. And you can continue with your practice and the repaying of your loans. . . .'' He grinned at her. ''Unless you beg for my help, of course.''

Lani had to smile. ''Maybe it really will work.''

''Of course it will. I've been dreaming about you since I first saw you—scrambling on the floor of the airport, picking up all that stuff from your purse.''

"Which *you* caused me to drop," she reminded him.

Surprisingly, Derek found no reluctance in admitting his weakness. "It was my knee—it gave out just as I reached for Mama's bag—ah, Charles's bag."

Lani lay her hand on his. She didn't have to say anything. He knew she was offering her love and support.

They sat smiling at each other for several heartbeats.

"So . . . Tell me you'll marry me."

Lani took a deep breath. "Yes. I will."

Derek stood then, bringing Lani up and into his arms for a long congratulatory kiss.

When he released her, Lani was warm and flushed and prettier than ever.

"Let's go tell Uncle Charles and Barbara."

Leaving the teapot and cups scattered over the table, she led him from the room.

Epilogue

Christmas Day dawned clear and bright, with the sun shining, just as the song says. Amid cheerful greetings of "Mele Kaliki-maka," Cyrilla rushed about the crowded house, seeing to last-minute arrangements. An hour before the noon ceremony, Larry found her in the kitchen, wearing her old, faded, around-the-house muumuu and overseeing the luncheon preparations.

"Mommy," Larry addressed her in the familiar way they'd adopted years before when the children were little. "You leave these people be. Get on back to our room and get dressed." He gave her a fond smile as he shooed her down the hall. "You don't want to be late for Lani's wedding."

"I won't, I won't." She hurried toward her room, detouring at the last minute to pop into Lani's instead.

"Mom, you're not dressed." Outwardly calm, Lani's rising voice showed the true state of her nerves.

"I just have to put on my dress," Cyrilla reassured her. Her eyes teared as she gazed at her daughter.

Lani wore a white satin *holoku,* specially made in a great rush by a second cousin who was a seamstress. Her dark hair was worn loose, the thick strands curling over her shoulders. Long fragrant strands of *maile* and *pikake* sat in an open florist's box on the bed, the red and white Beauty of Maui quilt beneath it.

Cyrilla pressed a kiss on her daughter's cheek and opened the door. "I'll be back in a minute."

By the time Cyrilla returned, looking lovely herself in her pale blue muumuu, Barbara was with Lani, trying to keep the bridal jitters under control.

"You should see Derek. Calm as can be."

Barbara shook her head. ''He was more excited last night when we opened our gifts.''

Lani laughed, taking her soon-to-be mother-in-law's hand and admiring the diamond ring there. ''He was surprised, but I know he's happy for you and Uncle Charles. We all are.''

Cyrilla agreed. ''It's been years since I've seen Charles enjoy himself the way he has since he met you. You two are going to be very happy.''

A call at the door sent Barbara scurrying and moved Cyrilla to action. She took the long leis from the box, arranging them carefully over her daughter's shoulders. Then she took the head lei and set it across Lani's forehead.

Derek felt his breath catch in his throat when he saw Lani at the end of the aisle. The small church was all decked out with bright red flowers for the Christmas celebrations. The Kalima family had added wide white ribbons and long twists of *maile,* and more white orchids than he'd ever seen before.

But the beauty of it all was eclipsed by the beauty of his bride. When Larry handed her over to his care at the altar, he felt another catch in his throat.

Lani's dark eyes met his, blue today with barely a trace of gray. The love that shone between them was so palpable the minister sighed. Then he began the words of the ancient ceremony.

"Dearly beloved . . ."